PULPOLOGY

PULPOLOGY

BY

D. ALAN LEWIS

PHILLIP DRAYER DUNCAN

JOEL JENKINS

EDITED BY LOGAN L. MASTERSON
AND MORGAN MINOR

PRO SE PRODUCTIONS
2014

PULPOLOGY
A Pro Se Productions Publication
Copyright 2014

The stories in this publication are fictional. All of the characters in this publication are fictitious and any resemblance to actual persons, living or dead is purely coincidental. No part of this publication may be reproduced or transmitted in any form or by any means, graphic, electronic, or mechanical, including photocopying, recording, taping or by any information storage or retrieval system, without the permission in writing of the publisher.

Edited by – Logan L. Masterson and Morgan Minor
Editor in Chief, Pro Se Productions –Tommy Hancock
Submissions Editor – Barry Reese
Director of Corporate Operations – Morgan Minor
Executive Officer – Fuller Bumpers
Cover Art by – Martheus Wade

Print Production and Formatting by David J. Foster
E-Book Design by Russ Anderson

Pro Se Productions, LLC 133 1/2 Broad Street Batesville, AR, 72501 870-834-4022
proseproductions@earthlink.net
www.prose-press.com

Pulpology

"The Snake and the Black Wolfe"
Copyright © 2014 D. Alan Lewis

"The Fallen Protector of Man"
Copyright © 2014 Phillip Drayer Duncan

"The Athena Palladium"
Copyright © 2014 Joel Jenkins

TABLE OF CONTENTS

THE SNAKE AND THE BLACK WOLFE by D. Alan Lewis	1
THE FALLEN PROTECTOR OF MAN by Phillip Drayer Duncan	34
THE ATHENA PALLADIUM by Joel Jenkins	79
ABOUT THE AUTHORS	110

The Snake and the Black Wolfe

D. Alan Lewis

Copper Hill, TN
1932

THEIR SMILES DISAPPEARED as I stepped from my car and looked around the small hick town. Only a few folks milled about the street and storefronts, but their white faces glared at me with fear or hatred, maybe both. One woman stopped in the middle of the road. She turned and with outstretched arms herded the three children who'd been trailing her like ducklings back the way they'd come. Either this bunch of hillbillies rarely saw a man of color, or they'd never seen one with decent clothing driving a new car. Either way, I didn't care.

After hours on the road in the August sun, my mouth felt as dry as the sun-baked dunes of Arabia. My clothes, however, were soaked. I pulled a handkerchief from my back pocket and dabbed away the beads of sweat from my bald head.

The local police station lay a few doors down. A couple of officers stepped out to see who'd arrived. Visitors must be rare in these parts. Only the copper mine drew people here. The few black men around here wore miner's helmets and a pound of dust compacted into their work clothes.

"Dat's a nice lookin' car ya got there," one of the deputies said as I approached. "Where'd ya steal dat car, boy?"

Reflexively, my fingers curled into fists. I could handle insults, but 'boy' wasn't a name I liked hearing, especially from someone that I could crush with little effort.

"I'm looking for the sheriff."

The deputy and his friend stepped closer and blocked the door.

"I don't think ya heard me, boy. Now where'd ya steal them fancy clothes and dat car?"

I really didn't need a fight with the locals, but this guy seemed all too willing. My eyes narrowed and the anger that brewed inside began to show. The smirk he wore faded and his hand nervously tapped the butt of his revolver.

"Leave'em be," said the sheriff as he stepped through the open door and looked me over.

"We was just…" the deputy started but stopped when he saw the old man's icy stare.

"You Dexter Wolfe?" he asked. When I nodded, he continued. "Your friend Dietrich in Port Victoria called. Told me you'd be heading this way. Come in."

I followed him into the station, happy to be out of the sun. The room had the typical small town look. A hallway in the back extended out a ways and I could see the bars for several jail cells.

"That's a lot of cages," I said and nodded to the hallway.

"They're usually filled to the brim with drunk miners on the weekends." He muttered and let out a frustrated sigh. The dumpy man scooted himself around the desk and dropped into the chair behind it. With the massive spare tire he carried around his waist, I half expected the chair to splinter beneath him. The wood creaked but its seams held.

"You know why I'm here?" I said and pulled up a chair of

my own.

"All he told me was that you were looking for a black family, gone missing round here," he said. "Also said you were the strongest, meanest son of a bitch in Port Victoria. 'Black' Wolfe was what he called you."

I couldn't keep the smirk off my face. "That what he said? I guess he'd know."

"Have to admit, ain't never heard of a black private dick before."

"We all need a hobby," I said and then filled him in on the details. I had a client whose son, Jack Reed, along with his wife and son had left on a trip to Knoxville but never made it. I'd tracked their green truck to a nearby town and learned they'd been spotted heading in this direction.

"Green truck? Chevy?" he asked. When I nodded, he let out a low moan. "A couple of good ole boys came in yesterday in a green truck. Claimed they'd found it out on a loggin' trailing near Turtle mountain."

"Where's the truck now?" I asked.

"Parked out back." He said, and in short order we stepped outside.

I glanced through the truck's cab. Only a crinkled map lay on the bench seat. I had one in my car, but grabbed it. Faint pencil lines showed a wobbly path along the local roads from the Carolina coast to Knoxville.

"Can you make out what road they were on?" I asked and handed him the map.

He laid it across the truck's hood and studied it. After a couple of minutes, he produced a pencil from his shirt pocket and sketched out a few lines.

"This here," he pointed to the new lines. "This here's Turtle Mountain. Them boys said they found the truck here."

He made a star on the map and then drew a line from it. "This is an old loggin' trail. I'm bettin' that Reed and his kin took a wrong turn and got lost up in there."

"Is there any place in that area they could have gone?"

"Son, there ain't nothing up there exceptin' shiners and trees." He turned and his voice lowered. "Those moonshiners up there… they don't take kindly to outsiders, especially blacks. I honestly don't think you're gonna find 'em. If you go up in there, you're likely to get strung up yourself."

I nodded and understood the dangers. The locals were well steeped in the age-old bigotry that had haunted the South for centuries. As a city rat, I'd grown up with some measure of safety from the Klan. But out in these hills, it was an entirely different story.

"I got an old lady paying me good money to find her kin. But I appreciate the warning," I said.

He turned his head and spit. "Where they found the truck… that's the south side of Turtle. Just sayin' that for as long as anyone can remember, folks that wander up in them woods tend not to come out. Gotta gun?"

I nodded.

"Keep it loaded and keep it close."

AFTER AN HOUR of driving the dirt roads, my legs felt unsteady as I stepped out of the car onto the grass-covered mountain trail. Deep weather-worn gouges lined the would-be road, showing that large trucks or wagons had used it repeatedly in the past. If I'd read the map correctly and driven the right distance, the Reed family had abandoned their car here. From the amount of crushed grass, there had been a fair amount of activity here recently. The good ole boys, as the sheriff called them, accounted for some of it.

The Snake and the Black Wolfe

Instinctively, I reached behind me and lightly tapped my holstered pistol. A brush with death many years ago had taught me to always double check the availability of my weapons. My pistol and hunting knife, as well as a pair of throwing knives on each ankle, were in place and ready should I need them.

The thick vegetation along the road offered only a few spots for someone to pass through into the woods beyond. It only took a few moments to pick up a trail. Three sets of footprints moved off into the woods. One of them may have needed a bathroom break and stopped here to find a suitable tree. I walked up the wooded hillside where the tracks led me.

Something else joined them. A fourth set of tracks appeared and from the size, he must have been at least seven feet with over three hundred pounds on him. There was a struggle and then only the giant's tracks moved off.

"Could he have carried them all?" I wondered out loud as I followed the ruffled leaves and kicked up soil the giant had left in his wake.

Crunching leaves in the distance stopped me in my tracks. I felt someone's stare, someone's presence near me. My eyes scanned and the words of my grandfather echoed in my head. As a child of the city, my mother occasionally sent me to my grandfather's farm during the summer months. His hunting and tracking lessons had proved to be some of the most useful teachings I'd learned during those years.

Don't look for what you're looking for. Just look and let the animal's movement be what makes you spot 'em.

Sticks in the distance moved, and then I saw the eyes and the long head. The buck stood on an adjacent hillside and studied my movements to determine if I was a threat. A doe and fawn stood frozen, a short ways behind him. It'd been years since I'd seen deer and couldn't help but marvel at their beauty.

The buck's attention moved to something behind me and I heard the snap of a twig. My shoulders slumped as I twisted with a fist coiled back.

"Motherf–"

A massive hand wrapped around my left arm, lifted and threw me a dozen feet or so. Pain shot through me as my back slammed into the moss-covered trunk of a maple.

I heard his footfalls as he charged closer. My vision was blurred but his large image couldn't be missed as I scrambled to my feet. I stepped backwards and rubbed my eyes. When we were close enough for me to make out the details, I found myself unable to cope with what I saw.

At first, I thought the man wore nothing but a smoky gray jumpsuit, but as he moved into arm's reach, I saw him up close. His smooth body was free of clothing and shoes. His twisted face possessed only one eye, positioned in the center above a large, flat nose. His skin had an unnatural grayish luster and looked like unfired clay, as if he was a living statue.

His right fist fired at me like a gunshot. Since I was a child, my reflexes had always been far better than the average man's. Some said my agility and strength bordered on the supernatural. This was true, and I knew the reason why. Still, even with my speed, I couldn't dodge fast enough. His punch caught me and filled my world with hurt.

The distance I flew backwards didn't really matter. I just knew that I had to get up and get the hell away until I could figure out what was happening. Again, his footfalls warned of his charging approach.

His left hand swung around towards my head as I rose. But this time, fire would be met with fire. I came up with all the force I could muster and met his fist head-on with a left hook. The impact was explosive. Pain tore through my arm followed by lightning-hot jabs on my face and arm, like little knives slicing through my skin.

But the punch proved much worse for the giant. His fist and forearm shattered in a cloud of dust and razor-sharp shrapnel that struck and sliced me open in dozens of places. He staggered back a step and showed no evidence of pain, only surprise at the stub that stopped a few inches below his elbow.

The force of the blow had knocked me off balance, as well, and I stepped back. Glancing down, I saw that my hand and arm were a bloody mess. Clay splinters, like broken crockery, jutted from the back of my hand like petals on a flower. When my gaze moved back to him, I saw his right fist impact the side of my skull.

The world screamed and nothing looked right. A shadow moved in front of me and I took a swing but my misguided action only served to put me within his reach. A cold hand grabbed my leg and I was thrown into the ground with such force that all the air left my lungs.

As he lifted me a second time, I gasped for breath like a fish pulled from a pond. The rush of air filled my ears as he swung me up and over. When I hit the ground again, I didn't feel pain, only a chill as the blackness took me.

I'M NOT SURE what bothered me more when my eyes finally fluttered open; the beauty of her blue-gray eyes that held so much sadness within them or the dozens of snakes which erupted from her scalp and glared at me with bared fangs. I pushed my head back, deeper into the pillows beneath me. Her expression changed from concern to surprise and ended on annoyance. She sat back but kept a hand on my chest in a reassuring but forceful manner. I couldn't help but express my discomfort.

"You've had a long nap," she said. I couldn't place the accent but it held hints of Eastern Europe. "Know that I mean you no harm. You are safe and your wounds have been tended to but they require more time to heal."

I lifted my wounded hand but something stopped it. I pulled my head up and saw that black leather straps held both wrists in place at my sides. I couldn't see my ankles, but felt straps around them as well. I looked back at my hand and found it wrapped in a thick layer of bloodied bandages. I flexed my fingers and instantly regretted it as waves of sharp pains rippled up my arm.

"One cannot be too cautious," she said and moved to the side in a way that didn't make sense until I got a better look at her.

My jaw dropped as I studied her. She was myth, a story I'd learned in college. She was Medusa. From the groin up, she had the body of a beautiful young woman. She wore nothing and showed no concern or modesty about her brazenly exposed breasts. Rippled muscles in her arms and stomach gave me pause to wonder.

The body of a snake emerged from where her legs should have been and stretched out across the room. Brown and green scales ran its length and merged with her dusky skin. Her head was crowned with at least a dozen small but very active snakes which jutted from her skull and moved with a life of their own.

She moved close again and hovered over me. As I looked into her eyes, I forgot about the snakes. Her round face held a majestic beauty with rich, full lips and a petite nose. Her hauntingly blue eyes took my breath away.

She pushed herself down against me and our lips met. She worked the kiss with a desperate passion and despite the feelings I had for my girl, Roxie, I couldn't help but enjoy the sensation.

The snakes had the hair on my body standing at alert, but the warmth of her lips and the movements of her tongue in my mouth made something else stand upright. Her hand brushed my cheek as we parted and a contented sigh escaped her.

"You love me, don't you?" she whispered as if we'd always known one another.

"Umm… We just met," I said and watched a look of disappointment appear.

"You - you don't love me?" she stuttered, and pulled away from me. She tilted her head and pondered something momentarily before a quirky smile appeared.

"Let me get you something." She turned and moved with surprising speed across the room to a cabinet-like piece of furniture. A number of bottles were snatched up and she carefully poured dabs from each into a small glass.

As she did this, I looked around the room and tried to conceive an escape plan. Her lair, as I thought of it, was huge. Large bricks made up the walls, but the ceiling looked like bare earth. The floor consisted of bricks as well, but these were well-polished. Colorful cloth banners stretched out from the tops of one wall to another. I felt a little like I was inside a large tent.

"Drink this." She approached and gave me a knowing look. "It will help you sleep a little longer and then we'll talk."

She held it out and the cup touched my lips, but I didn't sip the foul-scented fluid.

"I would imagine you think it is poisoned, am I right?" she said, and I glared through narrowed eyes at her. "If I wanted to kill you, you wouldn't have been brought here and you wouldn't have awakened."

The statement made sense to me. Why would she want me dead? I parted my lips and took a long sip. The bitter fluid immediately made my tongue go numb. My head spun and I fell back into the pillow. My eyes refused to stay open. I felt her hand on my cheek as she leaned forward and kissed me again.

"Damn!" I shouted and sat upright.

I raised my hands to wipe the sleep from my eyes and realized that the straps were gone as were the bandages on my left hand. I twisted my arm and examined it but there wasn't a scratch or scar.

I glanced around the room and was startled to see the giant staring back at me. He stood off to the side and watched. Only when I twisted and let my feet drop off the side of the bed did he show any sign of life. The Cyclops stepped forward and pointed to the door. A low rumble erupted inside of his chest before he opened his mouth and spoke.

"She will see you now."

His left arm sported a new hand. The appendage appeared darker and moist, like fresh clay. In all my years as a private dick, I'd seen some strange things. For that matter, my special abilities could be considered some of those strange things, but I'd never seen anything like this. Here stood a living statue who served Medusa.

The stone floor felt cold against my bare feet and my shoes were nowhere to be seen. Out of habit, my hand moved to the small of my back and tapped. The pistol was gone as were the other weapons.

My crumpled shirt lay on the foot of the bed. I snatched it up and pulled it on as I walked out the door. My stomach rumbled and a wave of nausea washed over me. It felt like I'd not eaten in days and wondered how long my naps had really been.

The moist air in the hall felt cool against my skin and held an earthy scent. I saw that we were underground as the hallway opened up into a network of caverns. Every ten feet or so, the yellow flames of oil lamps lit up the darkness and gave plenty of illumination for me to see. The stone Cyclops followed but kept a respectable distance.

I glanced back at him and decided to provoke something from him. My eyes moved to the new hand and I said, "Take it that your hand is doing better, too?"

He said nothing, but flexed the new fingers and grunted.

"I HOPE YOU enjoy the meal," she said and motioned to the table.

There were no chairs since the tabletop was only a foot off the floor. Colorful pillows were tossed about the room. I pulled a thick one to the table, sat and looked over the spread. Thick slices of roasted meat, venison I presumed, lay on a platter, surrounded by bowls of fruits and vegetables.

"I have to admit that I'm impressed. Most men are easily taken down by Theodotos." She nodded to the Cyclops. "But you stood your ground and broke his arm."

She lay back on her own pillow, across the table from me and waited. She nervously looked at the food and nodded for me to partake. My empty stomach growled as the scents filled my nostrils. Reluctantly, I took a slice of the meat and bite into it. The succulent spices made my mouth water and I ate it quickly. Without thought, I'd grabbed up a second then a third before I glanced up. Her smile lit up the room.

"I would imagine you have many questions," she said in a sexy voice that didn't sit well with me, not with all the snakes on her head watching my every move.

"You are Medusa?"

Her eyes narrowed, "No. But I see you know a little something about history."

"Then who are you?" I asked.

She twisted her face, which showed her annoyance, and then adjusted herself before she spoke. "My name is Nysa, youngest daughter of Medusa."

I searched my memories for the name. The Greek Mythology course that I'd taken at Fisk wasn't much help since the class started at 8 a.m. and my regular hangover kicked its hardest about that same time.

"You got your mother's looks, from what I know of my history. But… I thought she was… well to be blunt, ugly enough to turn men to stone," I said, and saw a hint of a smile encroach upon her full lips.

"Yes, she was cursed with a face so hideous that looking upon her would cause men to turn to stone," she said and sat upright. In doing so, a small and strangely sexy laugh erupted from her. "I'm aware that the story has been perverted over the years. Mother's beauty surpassed that of Aphrodite. Her parents were gods and had been cursed with two daughters of monstrous form. Zeus took pity and gave them what they wished for most, a beautiful daughter. Cursed by their heritage, Euryale and Sthemo were immortal, but Medusa was human, beautiful and mortal."

She pushed a plate of sliced fruit closer to me and then snatched up a pitcher and refilled the wine glass I'd already drained. "Please, eat. You need food to rebuild your strength."

"If I remember, your mother offended Athena in some way," I said, then lifted the wine glass to my lips. Before she could answer, I downed it all.

"Offended?" She huffed. "As a young woman, mother worshipped Athena. During her seventeenth year, the sea god, Poseidon saw her in the temple. Story is that he was struck by her beauty, but instead of wooing her, he raped her… there in the temple."

Her words became sharper as each one was spoken, and a growing uneasiness began creeping up my spine.

"That bitch Athena was so jealous that she cursed mother. Mother was defenseless, she struggled against the god that raped her… Athena blamed her and punished her by twisting her beauty and making her so repulsive that any man looking at her would be turned to stone. Poseidon said that mother's long blond locks had enchanted him. So, just to be even more cruel, Athena took mother's hair and turned her locks into snakes."

"But where did you come from? I mean, if she couldn't have a man around her, how did she get pregnant?" I asked.

Nysa took an apple from a bowl on the table and rolled it around in her hands. Her eyes focused on it and an expression of profound sadness came to her.

"Mother grew to hate men, all men. She escaped into the mountains and lived for years. Athena's curse meant that she'd never age. That bitch wanted mother to suffer. But many years later, mother encountered a man, lost in the mountains. He was half dead, but most importantly, he was blind. Mother took pity and cared for him. Without being able to see her, he didn't fear her. She told him about the curse, but he only cared about the kindness she'd shown him. They fell in love and he sired three daughters in as many years with her."

"What happened then?"

"Soldiers came to kill her, and father fell in the crossfire. After that, she never loved another man. Eventually, my sisters and I left to go our own ways. And you know the rest. Perseus showed up one day and took off her head."

I nodded slowly and felt the desire to hold her and pull away her sadness.

"I guess the curse was passed on to you and your sisters," I whispered, and watched her gaze move up to look at me.

"When we were born, Athena's rage couldn't be contained. She despised the idea that mother had found love, so she cursed us as well. We have the snake features, but not the hideous face. At least her youthful beauty was passed on to us. While mother's looks turned people to stone, it's love that does it for me."

Surprised, I sat up straight. "Is that why you asked if I loved you after we'd kissed?"

She smiled. "Yes."

I bit into a slice of apple and smiled at her. "What would happen if I did love you?"

Her smile disappeared. "Then you'd already be stone. Athena wanted to insure that our suffering was as great as mother's. Anyone who falls in love with us will turn to stone."

"I guess that makes you safer to be around than your mom," I quipped and noticed her stare turn icy.

"You know nothing…"

"Then enlighten me," I replied.

Frustrated, she glared at me. For a moment, I worried about being turned to stone or something else. Then I noticed her gaze move around the table and she nodded. This whole time, she'd not picked up a single morsel to eat.

"This food is wasted on me. I can eat it and enjoy it but it doesn't sustain my life or body. My curse… what my body requires as nourishment is the life force within mortals. Not just anyone, though… Only those who fall in love with me."

"I don't understand," I stammered, not sure what to think. "Where do you find… people?"

"I came to these lands, centuries ago. Occasionally, I'd go out and find the savages that lived in the hills. But it's too dangerous now, so I have Theodotos collect them when I hunger."

Her words struck a nerve. The reason I'd come to these hills returned to my mind: a missing family. I suddenly felt my stomach drop at the thought of explaining to Old Lady Reed that her family had been turned to stone by a mythical creature.

"How often do you need a meal?"

"I eat when I can and as much as I can. The bigger the meal, the longer I can go in-between feedings," she said with a devilish grin.

Before I could ask the next question, she cleared her throat and said in a whisper, "You are a beautiful man. I don't think that I'll tire of looking at you."

A fear crept up inside me. The terror of being turned to stone. A statue for her to admire for God knows how long. Would I be dead or trapped inside, forced to watch without any chance of escape or ability to let anyone know I was still there? That bothered me the most; the hell of being entombed within a stone effigy of myself.

Without thinking, I pushed aside all thoughts of her beauty and concentrated on images of my beautiful Roxie. She waited back home with those red lips that I loved to kiss.

"You have the divine in your bloodline," she said and bit her lip as she studied me. "I saw the birthmark on your…"

"I'm not divine," I said, and felt odd about her looking over my unconscious body.

"You don't understand. My kiss enslaves the hearts and minds of those my lips meet. Men, women, it doesn't matter. I have to kiss them in order to feed. I make them love me so that they willingly surrender themselves to my needs. They gladly give up their life so that I can live. Mother's looks turned flesh to stone but for me, they turn to stone when I draw out their souls."

Stunned, I pulled back and her eyes opened wide in panic.

The idea of Medusa's stone trick was one thing. For her, it couldn't be helped. She didn't hunt down men for sport. Nysa, however, killed to live. She didn't just hunt; she had her slave harvest the locals. This woman was every bit the monster that the legends made her mother out to be.

"No, please. Don't be afraid," she begged, and reached a hand out to me. "I... I can't hurt you. My kiss didn't work on you. Only someone whose blood is tainted... is touched by a divine bloodline could have resisted my love spell. Only someone blessed with godly lineage could have stood his ground with Theodotos."

Part of me wanted to explain that I wasn't the long-lost descendant of some Greek god. My strength came from a blood transfusion when I was a child. A superhero named Lady Victoria whose great powers had come from a chemical cocktail given to her during an experiment had given blood as a publicity stunt. By accident, the blood was given to me. My young and growing body accepted it, and was transformed by the chemical, as well. My strength, reflexes, and intelligence were all far above normal.

"What is he, by the way?"

"My protector. Created by my mother when I left to make my way in this world," she said and tilted her head in a playful manner. "When I have children, I'll make one for them as well."

My eyebrows rose and I didn't care for the look on her face, a playful yet hungry look. I refilled my glass and gulped downed the sweet-tasting wine.

She slithered around the table, wrapped her arms around me and pulled my lips to hers. The kiss, aided by the wine, awoke needs within me and I couldn't help becoming aroused. I pushed my lips back against hers and dug my fingers into her back, pulling her closer. Her kiss was intoxicating.

I felt a nipping at my ear and jerked back. The snakes on her head hissed and slithered around as if annoyed at what she was doing. Closing my eyes, I pushed myself away and took a deep breath.

"What are you trying to do? Make me love you with your kiss again?"

"No," she answered, and I felt the warmth of her fingers pulling my chin closer to her. I felt the small kiss she planted on my lips before she spoke again.

"No, that magic won't work on you. When I told you about my father, I didn't mention that his grandfather had been sired by a god. Only someone of divine lineage can sire children with us."

I opened my eyes and saw the twinkle in hers. It suddenly made sense why I was still alive.

"You want me to sire a child with you?"

She bit her lip and nodded. "I know this is strange to you…"

"Strange? You… you're something straight out of a book on mythology? You've got snakes watching me while we kiss…" I stammered and needed a way out of this, at least for a little while. "Look, this is some strange stuff that's going on here and I need a little time to… to digest what you've said."

I watched her move back with a disappointed expression. She nodded and returned to her side of the table where she lay back down. Her gaze never left me, though.

"I do understand. I had just hoped…" Her voice was low and melancholy. "I've waited centuries for a man to come along that I could be with."

She slowly sat up and moved to place her elbows on the table and her head in her hands. "Forgive me if I'm impatient. I know very little about courtship."

I nodded and she picked up a thin slice of the venison. "Eat and tell me about yourself. I want to know all about you."

WITH THE MEAL over, Nysa showed me the wonders of her home. The natural caves in these hills made a perfect home, and the natives made perfect meals. She explained how she'd lived openly for centuries before the Europeans arrived. In time, the hills in the region were heavily populated and eventually mined for copper. The new mineshafts opened more space for her home to expand. She'd enslaved one of the mine's foremen and used him as a means of keeping a steady supply of men coming into the depths of her lair where they'd be harvested. But the constant disappearances caused the mines to be shut down and abandoned.

We walked from cave to cave, room to room. Treasures, some thousands of years old, littered her lair. Paintings, statues and exquisite furnishings reflected the outside world in to her underground prison. That's how I saw this place: an over-done prison.

We ended in her bed chambers, although there was no bed. For hours, the conversation continued as we exchanged views of the world, old and new alike. When Nysa told me that I'd been out for three days, I understood the reason for my endless need for food and drink. It was the drink that was the problem. The only fluid available was wine and I'd downed far too much. Drinking had never been a problem for me, but this wine had a wicked punch. Eventually, my head began to spin and my speech slurred. Amused by my condition, she moved to my side, smothered me in kisses and helped me onto a pile of massive pillows near the back wall.

A strong scent rose of them, but it wasn't unpleasant. It reminded me of a spicy musk cologne. The air was permeated with her intoxicating scent. Nysa's long tail coiled around my feet and calves and she lay beside me. The closeness of her coupled with the smells only added to my conflicted arousal. Her fingers gently played with my hair and her lips gently kissed my face. Eventually, her head relaxed against my shoulder and we fell asleep.

HER ABRUPT SHOUTING woke me and I lifted my dizzy head to see what the commotion was all about. She rolled and thrashed about nearby. Arms lashed out at unseen enemies and her tail whipped around furiously.

"No. Stop it!" She cried out in a weak, tired voice.

I could see that her eyes were closed and realized that she was dreaming. No, not a dream, this was a nightmare.

"You can't leave me." She called out and thrashed around, repeating the words over and over.

She jerked around and came closer to me. I jumped to a crouching position and stepped carefully along the outer walls until I was near the doorway. My concentration was so focused on her, that I'd missed the cyclops who stood next to the exit.

He stepped away from the wall, blocking my path. He didn't breathe or make a sound, but just seemed to appear. My heart skipped a beat and I jumped back a foot.

"Jeezzzus," I whispered and realized that my right fist was cocked back, ready to launch at him. Since my childhood, no one had been able to sneak up on me. This creature gave me the first shock I'd felt in years.

He looked down at me with cold stone eyes and didn't move an inch. I considered my options and knew another fight wouldn't be advantageous for either of us.

"Does she usually have nightmares like this?" I asked and wondered if he had the mental capacity to really understand.

"When she sleeps, the souls within her torment the lady," he said in a deep rumble.

My mouth dropped open a little. I didn't expect an answer and I wasn't sure what to make of it.

"Souls within her?" I asked, and watched him nod. "I thought that she ate them… consumed them."

He remained still as I looked back and watched her. She mumbled to her unseen tormentors while thrashing about. A twinge of sadness struck me as I thought about her spending every night tortured by her memories or nightmares or worse, her victims.

"I don't want to stay in here while she is like this," I said and looked for a reaction. "Mind if I go back to the room I woke up in?"

He stepped to the side and said in that low rumbling voice, "The exit is sealed and impossible for you to unlock."

"You sure about that?" I asked, but he only stared blankly.

I nodded and stepped passed him. My feet moved slowly as I quietly stepped from the room. Once in the hallway, my pace quickened and I found the room I'd been in earlier. Another passageway which we'd not explored during the tour led off to the left. Glancing back to make sure I wasn't followed, I took the new direction and decided to check things out.

Sparsely hung oil lamps gave off enough of a glow for me to see the man-made tunnel. Wood beams stood packed against the walls and crisscrossed the ceiling. The hard soil of the floor felt cool against my bare feet and I silently cursed my lack of shoes. A pair of other tunnels moved off to the right, but I decided to keep on my original course. The further away I got, the more the air became thick and permeated with the moist smells of mold and decay.

The tunnel opened up in to a vast cavern that looked to

be the size of a sports stadium with me at the top level looking down into it. As I moved in, my gaze fell upon the acre-wide pit. The floor of it had a strange texture and I couldn't make out what I saw.

Grabbing one of the oil lamps from the wall, I stepped to the edge. The angle of the pit's walls and its rough surface would make for easy climbing. Slowly at first, I inched my way down but found the bottom wasn't as far away as I'd first thought.

A soft breeze blew over me and its cold touch made the hairs on my arms and neck stand upright. I jerked my head around and swore there were whispers somewhere in the vastness of the cave. I held the lamp back so that my eyes could adjust to the darkness. There was nothing to see except the stone walls and the blackness that the lamp's light couldn't reach.

I lowered myself down again but my foothold shattered beneath my weight. My hand lost its grip on the lamp as I frantically clawed at the rock face. My skin tore and nails broke but the fall could not be arrested. My body slammed onto a jutting rock and bounced off, dropping several feet onto the broken stones of the floor. Pain blasted into my skull as my head struck.

My body felt frozen to the core as my eyes fluttered open. The throbbing in my head hatefully reminded me of the fall. I lay still and moved my feet and arms to test for any breaks. Other than being sore, my body seemed intact. The lamp sat somewhere behind me since I could make out some glimmers of light off the rocks.

I rolled over and saw a woman, eyes opened wide in terror and mouth hung open in a wordless scream. Her outstretched arms reached out to me and the tips of her fingers lay a fraction of an inch from my face. I sat upright and pushed back away from her, only to see others reaching and looking at me.

I drew a deep breath as my eyes closed and I willed myself to relax. Nothing around me moved and the only sound was my pounding heartbeat. My breathing was fast and sharp at first but under control by the time I reopened my eyelids.

The light proved what the woman really was: a broken statue. Everywhere around and under me lay the shattered remains of stone men and women. This wasn't a cave, it was a burial ground. Cautiously, I stood on the uneven stones and picked up the lamp. Stooping down, I held it so that its light shown on the stone woman.

No sculptor could have caught the details and intricacies of her face. Every hair, eye lash, and subtle line in her face was perfectly preserved. She'd been scared or in pain from the looks of her final expression. My gaze moved around and the sight was horrific.

The floor wasn't just littered with broken figures; it was thick with them. I lifted a few pieces and dug down through them but only saw more stone bodies. Her words echoed in my thoughts. She'd been here for centuries and there was no telling how many people she'd consumed. Hundreds, thousands, maybe tens of thousands were in this massive pit.

I looked back down at the woman and ran a finger along the cold, smooth stone that was her cheek.

"Don't take it personally. I'm always spooked by strange women." A sense of pity for her washed over me and I couldn't help but add, "I'm sorry this had to happen to you… to all of you."

As I stood and turned to wall, an arctic-like breeze engulfed me. I drew my shoulders up and arms close to me as I stepped to the wall and began to look for suitable hand holds.

A distinct belief that I was being watched grabbed hold of

me. My need to escape this grave hastened my search for an escape route. I looked up and for the first time in my life, I yelped in surprise and shock.

The pale face of a child, maybe six or seven, stared back at me. She clung to the wall like a spider, with her head facing down and her eyes locked on me.

"Don't be sorry. It wasn't your fault." Her soft voice resonated through the room and held a childlike innocence. The voice had a distinct British sound to it, as well, and that's when I noticed her clothing. Torn and tattered, it still looked centuries out of date.

"Are… Are you really here?" I stammered and tried to take back control of my senses.

Her hand left the rock and she pointed off to a distance part of the chamber.

"I'm over there."

"I don't understand. Why are you here? Aren't you dead?" I asked and wondered how much a child would really know of the afterlife. Did she even know that she should have gone to wherever it is that a child goes to in the afterlife?

"Can't go nowhere," she said softly and then her tone changed to one of anger. "They say we're anchored here."

A bad feeling quickly replaced the creepy one I'd been experiencing. "We're?"

She pointed again and I turned to see a wave of people stepping towards me. Their arms reached out for me. Pleas for help, screams of horror, and curses were directed at the woman they loved.

I stepped back, unsure of what their intent really was. I quickly glanced up to the little girl but she wasn't there. Then I looked back at the approaching mob, but they, too, had disappeared.

I rubbed my eyes and reached back to the spot on my head where I'd landed on the rock. A knot had swollen up, but I didn't think the injury could have caused hallucinations. I dropped the lamp and started up the wall with as much speed and care as I could muster.

Upon reaching the top, I sat with my legs hanging off the side and thought about what I'd seen. For the first time in many years, my hands trembled. The climb had taken something out of me, but the whole nightmare had tilted my sense of reality. A creature from myth, a clay cyclops, and now, a pit full of ghosts.

AS I WALKED the tunnels back to her room, my ears picked up on something. I could hear the sound of crying. A small opening in the cave wall led me into another branch of this abandoned mine. Fewer lamps hung in this shaft and the air felt still and thick. A faint scent of urine grew stronger as I moved deeper into the shaft. Light from a distant lamp provided enough illumination to keep my path steady.

The crying turned into whimpering and lay somewhere ahead of me. I passed the lamp and saw its light glinting off of a series of bars along the right side of the tunnel. They formed a pair of large cages, just large enough for an adult. Huddled in the back corner sat a young black boy. His arms wrapped protectively around his face and head as if he tried to shield himself from the horrors of this world. After what I'd seen, I couldn't blame him.

"Hey, kid. What's your name?" I said in a low voice and then examined the lock.

His arms dropped and his wet eyes focused on me. Fear held his tongue for a moment until he saw that I wasn't made of clay and my skin was the same color as his. In a flash, he ran to me.

"Joey," he said.

"Joey Reed?" I asked, and watched him nod. At least one of the Reed family still lived. "Do you know if your mom and dad are still… still in the tunnels?" I didn't have the heart to ask if they were still alive.

"Da snake lady made them into stone." His words sent a chill down my back. The bitch had done that to the kid's parents while he watched.

It took some work, but the lock finally gave to my attempts to open it. I grabbed the boy up and started walking back the way I'd come. That still left me with a problem: finding a way out of this place.

We'd just made it back to one of the well-lit tunnels when the cyclops rounded a corner ahead and stared with those dead eyes. I lowered the boy to the ground and pushed him behind me.

"He is not yours to interfere with," Theodotos said and stepped forward. "The Lady will feast on his soul this evening when the moon is full."

His arms bowed out and his fingers curled up into fists. This lump of clay obviously had enough intelligence to see that I wasn't the type of man to allow a boy to be consumed. Plus, he had first-hand experience with me so he knew that I was strong enough and fast enough to be a challenge.

I couldn't help but smile. What he didn't realize was that I enjoyed a challenge. He'd taken me by surprise in the woods. I'd underestimated his capabilities. Now I knew and wouldn't make the same mistakes again.

"Run back a ways and stay down. If you see me go down for good, run like hell and don't stop, you hear?" I whispered to Joey.

The moment I heard him running away, I launched myself

at Theodotos. There was enough distance between us to get some speed up. He stepped back and pulled his right fist back. He planned on swinging as soon as I was in range but I had other plans.

At six feet away, I went in to a feet-first slide. His fist swung through the empty air, over my head where he'd thought I would be. My legs absorbed the punishment of the slide and I threw all my weight into a punch. My fist slammed into his right knee with a sickening thud. A sharp crack echoed back and forth down the tunnel.

A quick roll to the side got me clear of him and I was on my feet immediately. Theodotos tried to turn but staggered and fell against the wall. He looked at me, confused, and then down at his battered knee. The joint had been pushed backwards and cracks ran up and down his calf and thigh. For my part, I tried to open my right fist, but the attempt caused so much pain that I abandoned that idea. Blood poured from cuts on each knuckle and I knew that I had a limited amount of time before the numbness wore off and I started to feel the full effects of the damage.

We looked at one another and charged. He swung but I ducked and fired off a rapid series of jabs to his face with my left fist. With each impact I winced at the pain; after all, I was slamming my fists into living stone.

He ducked back and lunged. A hand grabbed my arm and he threw me sideways through the air, a dozen feet down the tunnel into the wall. I bounced off it and landed hard on my back. I thanked God that the tunnel floor was packed soil instead of stone.

I heard the thunder of his foot falls and rolled quickly as his fist came down where my head had just been. My feet got traction as I came up with an uppercut in to his jaw. Theodotos' head snapped back but before he could recover, I followed up with a vicious right cross. I knew the pain would be staggering but I threw everything into the swing. The impact devastated the cyclops as a cloud of dust and shards shot out in every direction.

His face and the forward half of his head had shattered. He staggered backwards, but swung his arms furiously. I couldn't tell if his swings were directed at me or were some sort of reflex movement. I sidestepped forward a couple of times as I judged the timing. When I saw the opportunity, I took another shot. This time, my blow shattered the remainder of his head. Theodotos fell back to the floor in a cloud of dust and didn't move again.

I DIDN'T KNOW where to go at first, but then remembered that I'd not been back to the room where I'd first awakened. During her tour, she'd kept me away from there. The boy in my arms said nothing and kept his head down.

"Could my weapons be there, or an exit?" I muttered out loud.

The boy clung to me tightly and didn't make a sound as I stepped lightly through the labyrinth of caves and tunnels.

What really bothered me was the possibility that I'd see her again. After an hour away from her, the fuzz that kept my thoughts fixated on her had cleared. Her kiss didn't enslave me but it did have an effect; her kiss and those damn beautiful eyes. I'd sat there and eaten with her, kissed her, and somewhere deep inside, I had wanted to take her and give her the children she wanted. I'd casually ignored the fact that she was a monster who'd have taken my soul if she could have. All the death and horrors had been justified, temporarily through the magic of her lips.

We turned a corner and found a tunnel that looked familiar. My smile and small laugh couldn't be contained. Joey pulled his head up and looked around but immediately buried it in the nape of my neck when her screaming began.

I wasn't sure if her shouts were her nightmares or if she'd discovered her bodyguard. It didn't matter to me because my destination was just through the door ahead. I only hoped that my guess was right.

The room had far more furnishings that I'd remembered. Chests and boxes sat piled high along one wall. My arm loosened its hold on Joey and he slipped to the floor.

I pointed to a corner and whispered, "See that cloth hanging down like curtains? I want you to hide behind it."

The distant screams were closing in on the room. My gaze darted from one spot to the next; gleaning every possible place my equipment could be stashed away. My skin itched as I thought about her catching me here without a pistol or knife. I felt naked without them, vulnerable. Worse, what if she found me and planted those red full lips on mine? It'd taken an army of ghosts to purge her mind-bending magic from my thoughts. I might not be able to resist or escape again.

It would be a matter of time before we'd be discovered, so I threw caution to the wind. Boxes, chest and cabinets were rummaged, their contents scattered about. Noise wasn't an issue anymore; speed was. I grabbed a pillow and slung it sideways without a thought but when it hit the wall, it made a muffled metallic sound. It was like lightly tapping your finger on a snare drum. I jumped and tore down the silk that covered the wall. As it dropped, I saw a brown and green hatch. A handle stuck from the right side of the huge copper door. Grabbing it, I tugged up and down but to no avail.

"Dammit," I shouted, louder than I'd wanted. Nysa wasn't

screaming any longer. Instead, she called out my name.

The door refused to give despite my tries but the harder I tugged the more the whole frame wiggled. Theodotos had been right; it would be impossible for me to unlock it. So, I did the next best thing. I slammed a fist into the wall, next to the door frame. Pain flashed up my arm but the stone loosened. Stepping back, I kicked hard several times until the mortar around it turned to powder and the stone fell away. I reached into the hole, grabbed the door facing and put a foot against the wall to push back. I strained and yelled as I felt my body pushed to the limit but finally mortar began to crack and give. In a chain reaction, one seam gave way and then another, allowing stone after stone to break loose around it. With a deafening crash, the copper door and frame broke loose and fell forward into the room, filling it with a thick cloud of dust.

"Joey!" I screamed, and the boy responded immediately.

He ran over and jumped on the fallen door and we both looked out into the darkness. In the distance, a hint of light dusted one side of the cavern. I grabbed his arm and pulled his attention to me.

"Listen, I want you to run. You hear me? I want you to run, get outside and find a hiding place. If I don't come out in a while, run and keep running until you find someone." I said.

His little head nodded but I could see the fear behind his eyes. After all he'd seen, I knew he was terrified. Nysa's calls were close and I feared it may be too late. There wasn't any doubt that she'd heard the door fall. Folks in China could have heard it.

"No!" she screamed, and we both spun around to see her in the doorway behind us brandishing a spear in her left hand.

"Go!" I said to Joey, but then realized he'd already darted into the darkness.

With surprising speed, she launched herself at the cave and him, but I grabbed her arm and pulled her to a stop. She spun and glared at me with a hateful expression.

"I need him!" she screamed, and then her expression changed and I could see the hints of lunacy in her crooked smile. "I need him… for the full moon. It's just a few days away. The soul of a child… the innocence will guarantee my fertility."

"He's a child, for Christ sake!" My words were harsh and she recoiled from me but then moved closer. The madness in her eyes and smile frightened me more than I thought possible.

"You'll love me, you'll see. It just takes time… these things take time." She stammered and moved close enough to reach out and let her empty hand brush my face in a gentle reassuring manner. "But we have to get him back."

She turned toward the cave, but I grabbed her right arm again. Nysa jerked it away and then slashed with the spear. I leaped back out of range of her hands but not her weapon. The tip of its head slashed my shirt and tore a thin gash across my chest. The back of my heels hit some of the loose debris and I fell. My upper back and head smacked the stone floor and bouncing stars filled my vision for a moment.

"I need him just like I need you," she said and let out a nervous laugh. "Theodotos can always be fixed. I'm not mad about that. I love you too much to let something like that upset me. We're going to be together and have lots of babies."

"At the cost of a little boy's life?" I said, and rolled onto my side.

My head pounded and I felt dizzy from the impact. A basket which had been knocked onto its side lay a few feet from me. My vision was blurred, but inside the basket I saw my boots, belts and my pistol.

The Snake and the Black Wolfe

"Maybe you can live with killing a child, but I can't."

I pulled my legs up under me and got up on to all fours. The move caused a wave of dizziness. My lips moved as I mouthed a silent prayer for my aim and for her soul. Then I dropped to the side, rolled and grabbed the pistol. I jerked myself up into a sitting position and aimed the weapon. I never heard the gun's report or felt it kick.

Part of me screamed out in horror as I looked into her eyes. Her expression was that of a young child who'd broken her favorite toy. Heartbreak and the terrible surprise that all you've wanted is suddenly gone.

A thin crimson line moved quickly down the center of her forehead, reached the bridge of her nose and streamed down the right side. Her eyes never closed, but stayed locked on mine. Her snake body rolled slightly and caused her torso to fall over to the side.

I sat there for a long while and stared into her lifeless eyes as well as the hole in her forehead my bullet had created. I couldn't stop the few tears that fell for her; after all, she'd been alone for so long. That kind of loneliness would have driven anyone mad.

A WEEK LATER, Old Lady Reed came to my office and picked up Joey. The hardest part of my job is the bad news. Telling someone their spouse is cheating is a cakewalk compared to this. I knew she'd never believe the truth so I'd come up with a story. A group of Klansmen had stopped the car and strung them up. In the South, that wasn't hard to believe. She took the boy and my handkerchief home with her.

I sat alone, unable to shake the heavy weight off of me until Roxie stepped into the office. Her desk was right outside the door and she'd watched and heard the whole thing. She already knew the true version.

She scooted herself up on the edge of my desk and looked down at me. I needed to see her round face framed by those golden locks, to see love in her eyes and not a monster's madness and obsession.

"You gonna be okay, Dex?"

"Yea, I'll be fine, doll," I whispered, and pulled her down into my lap.

My lips met hers, and, as always, my passion for her stirred within me. Suddenly reminded of the feeling that I'd experienced with Nysa, I opened my eyes and looked at my girl as we kissed.

With a moan of relief, I didn't see any snakes looking back at me.

The Fallen Protector of Man

Phillip Drayer Duncan

THE AX SPLIT the log effortlessly. The well-muscled man with the long strawberry hair and beard kicked it to the side. He grabbed another large log and set it in its place. He lifted the ax as though it were a toothpick, and again swung it down through the log in a single stroke. His fierce eyes were intent on their work, yet he showed no exhaustion.

"I've never seen anything like it, Hammer," said another man, sitting on a log nearby.

"What's that?" asked the large man with the ax.

The other man shrugged. "I've never seen anyone swing an ax like that."

"Yes you have," replied Hammer. "You've chopped wood with me on many occasions, Sam."

"Yeah," replied Sam, "but I've also never seen anyone work as hard as you do without breaking a sweat. Are you sure you're even human?"

Hammer laughed and glanced over where Sam rested on the log. Sam was obviously tired. His late twenties face was brimming with perspiration. His t-shirt showed large sweat stains around the neck and armpits.

Hammer, on the other hand, was dry and comfortable. They had been at it all day, yet he showed no fatigue. There wasn't even a trace of sweat upon his brow.

"Well, I can always stop, if you prefer?" chided Hammer.

Sam threw up his hands defensively. "Whoa there, big guy. Don't get all defensive on me. You know I couldn't do this on my own!"

Hammer gave him a good-hearted chuckle. The wood they cut today would keep Sam and several elderly neighbors warm over the course of the winter. Hammer really did have his own things that needed to be done around the house, but he knew that Sam truly couldn't complete this task alone. In reality, it would have taken a whole crew of men at least a week to get as much lumber as they had produced in a single day.

"C'mon now, Sam. These Arkansas winters aren't that bad."

"That can be true most years," replied Sam. "But the Ozark weather is finicky. You never know if it's going to ice, snow, or if the sun's gonna pop out."

Hammer smiled and chopped another log. He liked Sam. That was saying a lot because Hammer didn't like being around people. Sam was different, though. He didn't ask Hammer questions or try to pry into his life. They were friends, but Sam gave him his space. Hammer didn't really interact with anyone else, except when he had to.

Sam looked at the pile of split wood and said, "You know, I think we have another truckload already."

Hammer glanced around. "Yeah, I suppose you're right. Want to load it up?"

"Yeah," said Sam. "And I think this is the last one. We have enough."

"Are you sure?" asked Hammer.

"I'm positive. We chopped enough wood today for next winter, too."

Hammer nodded and started picking up wood and tossing it into the back of the truck. Sam stood up and joined him.

A few minutes later the bed of the truck was full and both men climbed inside the cab.

"So you gonna let me buy you a beer?" asked Sam.

"I really should be getting back to the cabin," said Hammer in the passenger's seat.

"Oh, come on, man!" said Sam. "It won't kill you to have one drink with me! You never go anywhere except the few times I've managed to drag you to the bar for a couple of hours."

"I don't know," said Hammer.

"Oh come on, you damned hillbilly recluse," said Sam, smiling. "Just for an hour! I promise you the people won't bite."

"All right, Sam, I'll join you for one drink, but that's it," replied Hammer with a sigh. "You know I don't like people."

"No," said Sam. "I know you don't give people a chance."

"What about you?"

"Except me," said Sam. "Lucky me gets to be BFFs with the scary ginger giant!"

"I don't know what BFF is," said Hammer. "So I don't understand your insult."

"Oh for crying out loud! It means best friends forever, I think. Something the kids say these days. You are so backwoods you can't even get my sarcasm!"

"You may be right about that, but I do know one thing."

"What's that?"

"You don't want to unload this wood alone."

THE SUN HADN'T finished setting yet, so the bar was mostly quiet. But there were still more people there than Hammer cared to be around. Most people eyed him warily, but some of the more inebriated tough guys eyed him challengingly. Hammer had never understood how, at every small dive bar, there always seemed to be at least one regular that seemed to want to flaunt their king of the hill status in any newcomer's face. As if the bar were their castle, and they needed to maintain dominance in the eyes of their serfs. Silly people, thought Hammer. This was another reason Hammer didn't like being around people.

They sat at the bar and Sam ordered drinks. Sam knew Hammer's preference and ordered him the darkest and strongest ale they had. Hammer thought it tasted like watered-down piss compared to what he drank in the Old Country. And he could never understand the need to keep it so cold, but he wouldn't complain. Not after last time.

Though he had nearly forgotten his old life, there were some things that stayed with a man. For Hammer, one of those things was to always spot potential threats. In one corner of the bar was a group of five bikers playing pool. Three of them were focused on pool. One was large and loud, making obnoxious comments and throwing his weight around. Occasionally he threw a glance at Hammer. Hammer knew that man could potentially be trouble. The fifth man was quiet and tucked away amongst his group. He, too, would occasionally throw a glance toward Hammer. Hammer knew that, like him, the man was simply scanning the room for potential threats. Hammer knew he would have no trouble with this man. Man number four, however, would be the one that would try to pick a fight.

"Ham?" Sam said, breaking into his thoughts. "Did you even hear a word I just said?"

"Sorry," said Hammer sincerely. "You know how I get around crowds."

Sam glanced around the near empty room. "Crowds? Geez, man. If this is a crowd, skip the fair this year, alright?"

"I always do," said Hammer with a shrug.

Sam shook his head. "So anyway, I was trying to prep you for the ladies walking towards us. They are almost in earshot so I'll be quick... Don't mess this up. I told this chick to bring a friend for you."

"What?" asked Hammer. "Why would you do that?"

"Because you're as uptight as an oak tree, man!" said Sam indignantly. "I'm trying to help you! You need the kind of attention only a female can provide, buddy."

"I'm not..."

"Listen, it's easy, pal!" said Sam with a grin. "Because these gals are easy! It's a sure deal. All you have to do is not mess it up, and the majority of your problems will be gone by morning! Trust me... And here are the lovely ladies! My, don't you both look absolutely stunning tonight!"

"Hi Sam," said one of the ladies. "This is my friend Heather."

Hammer was furious, but he passed a glance over the ladies anyway. They were pretty attractive women; that was no lie. He hadn't been with a woman in ages, and his groin ached from the need. However, being with one tonight wouldn't solve all of his problems, because as far as he was concerned, he didn't have any. At least he didn't have any today. He liked his solitary life. Sure it was lonely more often than not, but he was content. No one bothered him, and he didn't hurt anyone. That was how he preferred it. Sam should have at least said something to him before pulling a stunt like this.

"Heather, it's a pleasure to meet you! Missy said you're a cool chick!" said Sam, gently shaking the woman's hand. "And this giant ball of happiness beside me is my friend Hammer!"

Heather gave him a seductive smile and said, "Hammer, huh? That name indicative of something?"

She dragged the word *indicative* out so that it was quite

obvious what she was asking. Hammer glanced over at Sam who was mouthing the word 'easy' at him. Hammer shook his head and said, "No. It isn't."

There was an awkward silence for a moment, during which Sam shook his head in disappointment. Hammer shrugged.

Sam broke the silence, saying, "So, ladies, let me order you a drink!"

Hammer turned his head and looked away. His eyes fell on one of the TV screens hanging from the wall. One of the barmaids was flipping through the channels lazily in search of a bar appropriate sports channel. From behind him he could hear the obnoxious biker making comments about him. It wouldn't be long now, he thought.

He wasn't really paying attention to what was on the television, but something caught his eye just before the channel flipped again.

"Hey! Wait!" he yelled at the barmaid. "Could you please flip it back, miss? Just for a minute."

The barmaid said, "Back to the news?"

"Yes, please," said Hammer.

From behind him, the loud biker said, "Hey, we want to watch the game!!!"

The barmaid looked uneasy.

Hammer met her gaze and said, "The news, please. Just for a minute."

She nodded and flipped the channel back to the news.

"Also, turn it up, please." said Hammer.

She complied and the news anchor's voice became audible. "This gang is practically taking over the country, and law enforcement agencies aren't taking any real action against…"

"Seriously, Hammer? The news?" asked Sam.

"Shhh," was Hammer's only reply.

"There have been shocking reports about this gang with the strange name. They call themselves Ragnarok Begins. Now get this! Apparently Ragnarok is the word for the apocalypse of Norse mythology! Is this gang trying to bring about some kind of apocalypse? Did you know..."

"Why are you so interested in this?" Sam asked. "Everybody has heard about Ragnarok Begins. It's been in the news for weeks!"

Hammer spun his head back toward the television.

"Yes, it appears it's a largely connected criminal enterprise that is growing by the day," said the reporter.

Hammer's attention was interrupted again by the loud biker.

"I said we want to watch the game! Change it back before I come up there and change it myself!"

Hammer could tell the voice was getting closer. The man was approaching from behind. Hammer focused on the TV.

"They have people in nearly every city, but their home base seems to be in Little Rock Arkansas, of all places. They have a large building there that is referred to as Key, or Key Tower..."

"Listen, you hillbilly..." interrupted the biker as his hand fell on Hammer's shoulder.

In a blur of motion Hammer spun and punched the biker. It sounded like a gunshot, followed by the sickening crack of breaking bones. Everyone stared at him with horror. The biker lay on the ground with blood pouring from his nose and mouth. He didn't appear to be conscious. Hammer turned to face the TV again.

"Little is known about the man leading this gang, but he goes by the name Lock," said the reporter.

Hammer turned to look at Sam. Sam, along with the entire bar, was still staring at him in shock after what he had done to the biker.

Hammer's voice was little more than an angry rasp when he said, "I've got to go."

"Jesus, Hammer!" cried Sam. "What about him?"

Hammer shrugged. "Call an ambulance."

He headed for the door.

Sam followed him outside. "Hammer! What's wrong? Where are you going?"

"Little Rock," Hammer said without looking over his shoulder.

"Little Rock?" asked Sam, "Why? Because of that gang stuff on the TV?"

"Yeah," said Hammer coldly. "I've got to stop him."

"Lock and his Ragnarok Begins? What's any of that got to do with you?" asked Sam.

Hammer turned to face Sam with fire in his eyes. "He killed my father."

HAMMER MADE IT home and started packing. Sam stood awkwardly in the living room, trying to talk some sense into his friend.

"Hammer, I don't understand, man. How can you know that this guy killed your father?"

"I just know, all right?"

"Well, he's still going to be there tomorrow, man. You need to slow down and think about this. I mean, we could spend tonight with the ladies and set out for Little Rock first thing in the morning."

"No, I can't. I have to go now. Every minute I wait he gets stronger. I should have done something a long time ago. I didn't. I'm not going to make that mistake twice," said Hammer. After a pause he added, "What do you mean we?"

Sam shrugged. "Well, obviously I'm going with you."

"No, you aren't." said Hammer as he pulled his handgun out of the closet.

It was an old 1911 model .45 that he had had a very long time. It would do.

Sam eyed the gun warily, "Yes, I am! And I'll tell you why. For starters, you are acting just a wee bit crazy and someone needs to be watching out for you. Secondly, you don't know Little Rock. How are you even going to find this guy?"

Hammer thought about it momentarily. "I don't know. I'll figure something out. I know him better than anyone."

"That may be true, but I have friends there. People we can trust to help you on your little quest."

"Fine," said Hammer. "You can come. But don't get in the way when things go down."

"I won't. Believe me." Sam paused and said, "What exactly are you planning to do?"

Hammer didn't bother answering, but slid the clip home and headed for the truck.

DURING THE LONG car ride, Sam had lots of questions. But Hammer didn't feel like answering. His mind was elsewhere, visiting the recesses of his memory. He remembered that fateful day when Asgard fell. It wasn't a dark force that had destroyed his home. Humans switched their allegiance to another deity. Without the prayers and sacrifices of the faithful, the Norse gods began losing their power. Soon, Asgard began to crumble. The gods were forced to roam the earth, weakened by the loss of power. They were still immortal, but their powers were mostly gone.

Loki had taken this opportunity to get back at the gods, namely his adopted brother Odin. In their weakened state, no one expected an attack. He did, however. Hammer, who was once called Thor, tried to save his father, but Loki was prepared. With his powers gone, Thor couldn't wield his mighty hammer. Loki had taken it from him, and laughed in his face. His uncle made him watch while he killed his father.

It was a horrific scene for all of the gods. Loki struck down any who opposed him, and the gods dissipated. They were the Norse gods no longer, they were just immortal men. They each went their separate ways. With no hope or allies, Thor gave up his mantle as the Protector of Man and disappeared. He wandered the world alone, always watching for a sign of his uncle. Loki was never anywhere to be found. After several hundred years of looking, he had eventually settled down in a small cabin in the hills of the Ozark Mountains. He had been there ever since. He had given up any hope of ever finding his evil uncle.

Loki had reappeared. There was no way that it wasn't him behind the Ragnarok Begins gang. Ragnarok was supposed to be the Norse version of the apocalypse. The humans had believed in it, but it had never come to be. Loki's message was quite clear. He wanted to bring about the end of the world. He wanted to throw it into chaos.

So be it, thought Hammer, so long as I get my revenge.

CONSIDERING HOW LITTLE planning he had done, Hammer was pleased with how well things were going. When they arrived in Little Rock, Sam had contacted some friends. They had been given a place to stay and even found some information about Lock.

Apparently, Lock had a stronger following than what the news had reported. It was commonly believed that the entire police force and all city officials were under his payroll. Lock was the unofficial city mayor. No one loved him, but there were so many that were highly loyal to him, he had virtually no opposition. Lock didn't have to worry about having large security guards with him everywhere, because no one dared attack him.

They had learned that Lock was known to visit a city park nearly every day. It was an unspoken rule that when Lock visited the park, he was to be left alone. Criminals, police, and even most civilians knew that. Bothering Lock while he was sitting on the park bench was the fastest way for a person to get themselves into a heap of trouble.

Fortunately for Hammer, he wasn't concerned about getting himself into trouble. He went and hid near Lock's bench. Killing his uncle in a park would gather a lot of attention, but it would be much easier than trying to storm Key Tower. He knew he would likely end up in prison, but what did that matter? He spent his life alone in a small cabin anyway. He didn't figure a jail cell would bother him. The forty or fifty years he might face was but a grain of sand compared to the time he had spent wanting his vengeance.

Hammer glanced around him. There hadn't been a sign of Lock yet. A small part of him was nervous. He had been waiting for this day for a very long time. He had thought about killing Loki a thousand different ways over the years. Back then, guns had yet to be invented. He still wasn't completely sure that it would kill him.

He heard a voice nearby. He tucked himself low and listened.

A man's voice said, "You may go now. I wish to be alone."

"Yes sir, Mr. Lock," replied another man's voice, and Hammer heard the footsteps indicating his departure.

He glanced through the bush where he was hiding. The

man Lock was wearing an expensive-looking black suit. He appeared to be in his early thirties. His hair and features were dark, and his face was handsome.

There was no way for Hammer to verify that it was Loki for sure. He realized that as he stared at the man. If Loki had been able to retain even the smallest bit of his power, then he could look like anyone. That had been the greatest of Loki's powers. He wasn't just a master of disguise; he was a shape shifter.

It didn't matter, Hammer reminded himself, and either way this man was evil. He needed to be stopped.

Lock sat down on the bench and stared out over the small duck pond in front of him. His back was toward Hammer. That was how he had planned it. Loki had never been easy to sneak up on, and Hammer didn't want him to know that he was coming.

Hammer surveyed the area. There didn't appear to be anyone in sight. That would make things even easier. If there weren't any witnesses, he might be able to get away with the murder he was about to commit.

Slowly, he stepped back from the bush, ensuring that he didn't make a sound. He began approaching the man's back. He moved each foot with care, making sure he didn't give himself away. He slowed his breathing, so as to not be too loud.

He was just a few feet away now. Slowly he raised the gun as he moved in. The barrel was only a foot or so from the back of Lock's head.

"That's quite close enough Thor," said the man without turning, "Excuse me... I guess it's just Hammer now. Is it not?"

"What?" said Hammer, surprised. "How could you know–"

He was interrupted as he heard the clicking sound of a firearm being cocked right behind his head.

From all around he saw men approaching with guns. There

were five of them, then ten, twenty, and then he lost count. He was completely surrounded. Men were coming from all around now. Some were dressed in camouflage that had allowed them to blend in perfectly with their hiding spots. Others were simply dressed in suits. They were all armed with assault weapons.

"Drop the gun, Hammer," said a familiar voice behind him.

He turned around to find Sam pointing a handgun in his face.

"Sam?" asked Hammer.

Sam smiled.

Lock laughed and Hammer turned back toward him.

Casually, Lock stood up from his seat on the bench and turned to face him.

"It's been a long time, nephew. How have you been?" asked Loki with a broad grin.

"What's going on here?" asked Hammer.

"You never were very smart, were you?" asked Loki.

Hammer glared at him. "What have you done to Sam?"

Loki laughed. "I've done nothing to your dear friend. He's been mine all along."

"How can that be?" asked Hammer. "No, I don't believe you. You've done something to him, one of your tricks."

"Please, Thor," said Loki. "You and I both know that neither of us possess the power we once did. If that were the case, you wouldn't be toting around that firearm instead of your mighty hammer."

Hammer looked back at Sam. "Is this true?"

Sam nodded at him.

"My poor stupid nephew," said Loki with a grin. "You didn't really believe that I would have allowed you to go unchecked, did you?"

Hammer glared at him.

"Long before I ever put my plans into motion I knew that you would be a problem. I knew you had spent so many years looking for me. You were even close a few times. You spoke to me face to face on more than one occasion. It was like a little game for me. Eventually you gave up, though. I knew, however, that once I started my plans you would come knocking. So I sent Sam to be your friend. Someone you could come to trust over the course of a few years. I had to make sure that you subtly found out about my little plans, so I made sure he didn't tell you outright. Then it was just a matter of coming to this park everyday where I would be out in the open."

Hammer stared at him in disbelief.

"What? You didn't actually believe that I had become a lover of nature? You are just too predictable, nephew. I knew you would think this was the best opportunity. I made sure that Sam would help that idea along just in case. And, well, here you are."

In a single quick movement Loki ripped the gun from his hands. Defenseless, his hands were pulled behind his back by Loki's thugs.

"How does it feel?" asked Loki. "How does it feel to be so weak, nephew? You were once the mighty definition of pretentious. Today you are just a weak little man, like any other."

"You said you were weak, too," replied Hammer.

"No," corrected Loki. "I said that we both had lost our powers. I never said that I was weak. While you were whittling your days away in the woods, I was out here. I was learning. I was adapting. I've mastered every form of hand-to-hand combat. I've become proficient with every weapon. No, my nephew, I am not weak. I am now the most powerful of all of the gods. You can look down upon me no more. I am your better. And with you out of the way, there is no one that would dare oppose my plans."

Hammer spat on the ground. "And what exactly are your plans?"

"The name isn't obvious?" asked Loki. "Are you truly so dull? Ragnarok Begins didn't ring a single bell? I'm going to bring about the apocalypse. I'm going to take the little humans to war, and when it's all over I will be their god. The only god still standing. Humanity will bow to me and since I will be the only god, they will believe in only me."

"You want your powers back," growled Hammer.

"It's not just my power, you ignorant hillbilly! I will get all of the power! Every human on earth will believe in me alone. I will become more powerful than any of us ever imagined. And since I've got this whole immortal thing going for me, it should last... Well, forever."

"Why?" asked Hammer. "Why are you doing this?"

"You even have to ask?" Loki's smile changed to an angry glare. "You don't remember? You don't remember when you had me locked away because I angered the gods? Do you not remember whose entrails you used to tie me up with, dear nephew?"

Hammer hung his head. "It was..."

He paused.

"Say it."

"It was your son's." Hammer looked up into his eyes. "I'm sorry Loki. I truly am. It was wrong. This won't make it right."

"No," said Loki. "I care nothing for making it right. I care nothing for the gods. I want to see you all quiver beneath me."

"Fine," spat Hammer. "Then kill me and be done. I care not."

Loki's glared melted back into a mischievous grin. "You have no care at all for the human race, oh Protector of Man? Have you forgotten your mantle, Thor? You are supposed to be their protector. Yet you've done nothing for them! You've never been worthy of the title. Not then, and not now. You know they say that the Nazi swastika was designed in your honor! Yet you were hiding away throughout that whole war. They killed millions bearing a symbol dedicated to you, and you did nothing Protector of Man."

Hammer stared at him.

Loki continued. "I'm not going to kill you, nephew. I'm going to lock you away and make you watch. My only regret is that I don't know where your own sons ended up. Maybe someday I will find them, and then you will get the opportunity to know what it's like to be bound by the entrails of your own offspring!"

Loki punched him in the face. Hammer fell backwards, but his captors kept him on his feet. Loki punched him again, and he felt his nose break. He punched him again, and his lip split. He punched him over and over while cackling like a mad man. Hammer could feel the blood running down his face. He could feel himself slipping away.

Loki laughed in his face and said, "Do you remember that time I convinced you to dress up like a woman, so that we could pull a grand scheme to recover your hammer?"

Loki paused for a laugh. "This is going to be kind of like that but without the hammer this time. Your hammer has been long-lost and forgotten, oh mighty Thor. And it's the human race I'll be fooling. And you will only be watching. Enjoy the show, nephew!"

Hammer's last image was Loki's fist coming toward his bloody, swollen face again. Then all was darkness.

HE AWOKE IN a cell. His first thought was of Loki's face. He had beaten him again. He didn't feel any particular hurt pride over having been beaten. When he had still been a god he had been a very prideful man. He had been one of the most arrogant beings to ever exist. He wasn't now. After all that had happened and his years alone, he didn't concern himself with his own greatness. Mostly because he didn't feel like he was great. He felt like a failure. That part didn't even bother him. It was something else. It was something that Loki had thrown in his face. He was supposed to be the Protector of Man. Yet he was not. He hadn't been. Even when the title had been bestowed upon him he did little to protect mankind.

His face was sore and swollen. He slowly opened his eyes. He glanced at himself and felt his face. He had been bandaged and treated for his injuries. He sat up slowly and looked around.

He was in an old-style jail cell that was actually made of bars. The entire room was filled with jail cells, as though he were in a prison. Most of the cells had people in them.

They were wearing normal clothing, not prison garb. Most of them didn't appear to be in bad shape, though they all seemed miserable. There was a pretty woman in the cell nearest to him. She was staring at him. He nodded. She turned away.

A door on the far side of the room opened and several armed men entered, led by Loki. Most of the people in the cells began cowering away from him in fear. Hammer just stared at him.

"The god of thunder has awoken," said Loki as he approached the cell. "How do you like your new home Thor?"

Hammer glared at him.

"Awww," said Loki as though he were speaking to a child. "Is somebody being a gwumpy bear today?"

Hammer's gaze didn't falter.

Loki smiled. "I welcome you, my honored guest, to my home in the sky. Admittedly it isn't quite Asgard, but Key Tower is quite luxurious. Of course you wouldn't know that because you're stuck here. And as much I would love to give you the grand tour, I'd rather know you're down here rotting."

"You should have just killed me," said Hammer.

"Oh, poor, stupid Thor. Your suffering hasn't even begun. Don't start begging me for death already."

"No," said Hammer. "I mean that you should have just killed me, because when I break free from this cage I'm going to rip off your head and beat you to death with it."

Loki laughed. "Finally some life from the thunder god. Too bad it's too late. This, nephew, is my personal prison. A few humans have been foolish enough to oppose me, and this is where I keep them. You may wish to get to know them. You will be here together for a very long time."

Loki turned and walked away. Hammer glared at him as he went.

After Loki was gone, Hammer realized that the captives were staring at him. He glanced at the woman. She was staring at him, as well.

She said, "So, welcome. I guess we're trapped here."

Hammer nodded, "I guess so."

"Why did he call you Thor?" she asked.

"Because that was my name as he used to know it," he replied.

"He talked to you as if you were actually the Norse god or something."

Hammer nodded.

"Care to explain why?" she asked.

"You ask a lot of questions," he said.

"Well, I'm a reporter. Kind of goes with the territory," she said. Then, after a pause: "You don't recognize me?"

"No," he replied simply. "Should I?"

"Oh, well most do so I just assumed you would. I guess you're not from around here?" she asked.

"No," he replied. "I live up north."

"Oh, well my name is Deanna Carrie. I'm a reporter for the Little Rock Evening News."

Hammer nodded. "I guess you reported something that Loki didn't like?"

"Loki?" she asked.

"Sorry," said Hammer. "I meant Lock."

She looked at him thoughtfully but didn't say anything.

A tall broad-shouldered man with graying hair and an authoritative voice said, "He called you his nephew and he called you Thor. You accidentally called him Loki. Care to explain?"

Hammer looked at the stranger warily and said, "Who are you?"

The man responded, "Chief Graham... Or at least it was. I guess it's not anymore. I was the Chief of Police, but I wouldn't let Lock buy me. I didn't realize how much of my department he had already bought. Most of the other guys in here are other officers that didn't have a price tag on their loyalty."

Hammer nodded but remained silent.

"So are you going to answer the Chief's question?" asked Deanna with a sly smile.

Hammer shrugged. "I guess it doesn't matter much now. He called me Thor because that used to be my name. I called him Loki because that used to be his name."

"You expect us to believe that you're a Norse God?" asked Graham.

"I don't care what you believe," said Hammer simply.

"Wait a second," Deanna asked. "But I thought Thor and Loki were supposed to be brothers."

"A common misconception," replied Hammer, "Loki was my uncle. He was the adopted brother of Odin, my father."

"So, if you really are Thor, why don't you just break us out of here?" asked Graham.

"I don't have my power anymore."

Graham didn't say anything, but watched Hammer intently.

"How does a god lose his power?" asked Deanna.

"People stopped believing," said Hammer remembering once again. "As people lost faith, our powers dwindled, Asgard crumbled and we were forced to earth as little more than men."

"So where are the rest of the gods? Why don't they oppose him?" asked Deanna.

"Odin is dead," said Hammer with his eyes to the floor. "When we descended from Asgard. Loki betrayed us all. Where the others are, I do not know."

"I see," said Deanna. "So I guess that's it, then, with you being captured."

"No," replied Hammer. "That is not it. Whether any of you believe me or not is irrelevant, but I'll tell you this... I'm getting us out of here and I'm going to stop him."

Graham had a twinkle in his eye, and some of the other captives glanced over at him. Hammer knew he had succeeded in at least one thing. He had given them hope. It wasn't much, but it was a good enough place to start.

"So do we call you Thor?" asked Deanna with friendly smile.

"No," said Hammer. "I haven't been deserving of that name for a long time. It's not who I am anymore. It's not likely who I will ever be again. Just call me Hammer."

BREAKING OUT WASN'T going to be an easy task, but they had plenty of time to look over all of the angles. He didn't know if Loki had surveillance, and might be able to hear everything they said. Hammer wasn't quite as stupid as Loki thought. He might not be a genius, but he hadn't exactly spent all of the years in his cabin doing nothing. He, too, had spent his days learning. He started watching for any opportunity. The problem was that there just weren't any.

The locks on the cell were electronic, they couldn't be picked. The guards never opened the cells, but rather just tossed food through the gaps. There would be no way to try to grab one. There wasn't any feasible means of escape. It appeared that Loki wanted them to stay in their cells. Each cell was fitted with a toilet and bed so there was no need for them to go out. They didn't even get showers. Loki wanted them stuck in the cell with no chance to escape, and the bare means to survive. Loki just wanted them to survive. That had given Hammer an idea.

He walked over to his bunk. Quickly he ripped the thin sheet off and walked it over to the farthest corner from the door. He tied a tight knot around the bar.

Deanna stood up in her cell and said, "Hammer? What are you doing?"

"I've had enough," Hammer said with a somber expression. "It's hopeless. I don't want to live like this."

"Wait!" she cried. "Hammer, don't do what I think you are about to do!"

Quickly, he took the sheet a couple feet from the knot and tossed it around his neck.

"I'm sorry. I can't go on like this," he said.

"What about your promise?" she screamed at him frantically.

Hammer gave a bitter laugh. "What's the point? Loki's won! Can't you see? There is no hope! I'm not a god anymore.

I can't save you. No one even believes in me anymore."

"Wait, Hammer! No, Thor! I believe in you!" she cried, but it was too late.

Hammer kicked out his own feet and let himself drop to the floor, hanging by the sheet. His oxygen was cut off immediately and he started to choke. A siren went off somewhere and armed guards ran into the room. They quickly disengaged the lock and ran into his cell.

As the first of the men approached, Hammer shot up from the floor, ripping the sheet from the wall. He punched the first guard, knocking him unconscious immediately. He grabbed him by the throat and swung his other hand out to backhand another guard. He picked up the first guard and hurled his body over the heads of the others to land right in the cell door. It happened so fast that the guards outside of the cell didn't have time to react. They tried re-engaging the lock, but the first guard's body was now in the way.

Hammer was a blur of speed and power as he thrashed his way through the guards. He wasn't a trained martial artist, but he had spent his entire life fighting. The professional training and weapons of the guards couldn't match up to thousands of years of fighting experience. They fell before him one after another.

In moments he was out of his cage and beating the remaining guards senseless. More guards ran in and opened fire on both Hammer and their comrades. Hammer knew that Loki wouldn't risk the lives of his precious prisoners by giving his guards real guns. His assumptions were correct when the rubber bullets and bean bags started zipping by his head. He grabbed one of the guards and used him as a human shield. He scooped up a fallen gun and started returning fire. He was a huge man and the limp body of his human shield wasn't big enough to completely cover him. Rubber bullets cracked against his arms and shoulders. It only served to make him angrier. He charged, sprinting at his adversaries. When he was close he hurled his human shield forward knocking them from their feet. Before they could respond he was on them.

He ran out the door, the other prisoners cheering him on.

He found himself in a hall, at the end of which he could see the control room. He charged in and there were several more guards waiting. They stared at him in horror.

"Surrender or die," said the empty-handed prisoner to the armed guards.

They looked at one another and laid down their guns.

"One of you shows me the controls."

No one moved.

"Now!" boomed Hammer.

One of the guards reluctantly got up and walked over to the control desk.

"Release all the prisoners," Hammer said.

The man pressed a button and Hammer could see all of the doors open on the monitor screen. He watched Graham organizing men and gathering up fallen weapons.

"Now," said Hammer. "Open the door so we can get out."

"Oh man," the guy gulped. "Look man, Lock will have me skinned if I let you guys go."

"That may be," said Hammer. "But if you don't, I'll beat you to death right now. On the other hand, since you know that Lock is going to kill you for helping me, it seems to me that you boys only have one option that works out for you in the end."

"What's that?" asked the guard.

"Switch teams. Help us escape. Then I'll let you go. You can run away if you want."

"He'll find us," said the guard helplessly.

"No he won't." Hammer shook his head, "He's going to be too busy trying to find me to worry about you boys. Trust me. It's really your only option. Helping us get out of this building is the only way that you are going to survive. But I need a decision now. Live. Or die."

Graham came around the corner and Hammer waived him down.

The guards slowly started standing up and glancing around to one another. The first guard finally spoke up. "Okay, we'll do it your way."

Hammer smiled. "All right, let's go."

Graham asked, "What was that about?"

"We've got an escort out of this tower." He turned to the guards. "Where do we go from here?"

The first guard responded, "Out this door is an elevator. We are in the basement underground. We'll have to take the elevator up to the first floor."

"Lead the way," said Hammer.

Suddenly the radio started going off. It was Loki's voice.

"Status Report! Why are there alarms going off in my prison! I want a status report this instant!"

The guards looked miserable.

Hammer walked over and keyed the mike. "Status report... Your prison is mine now, dear uncle. I own it."

"Thor!" the voice spat back menacingly.

"Are you home, uncle? Are you here now in your precious tower? I'm heading for the top floor to say hello."

"You're going to suffer, Thor. I'm going to remove your arms and legs. I'm going to cut out your tongue. I'm going to make you spend eternity as a helpless vegetable! I'm going to make you watch while I tear your world apart!"

Hammer laughed into the microphone. "I'll see you on the top floor."

Hammer killed the microphone and headed for the door.

"What are we going to do?" asked Deanna.

Hammer said, "We're going to get out of here."

"But what about all that you said about going to the top floor?" she asked, confused.

"A ploy," said Hammer. "Loki thinks I'm an arrogant fool. And he's afraid of me. He's going to be calling every guard he's got to the top floor."

"So what are we going to do?" she asked.

"We're gonna walk right out of the front door," Hammer said.

"I STILL CAN'T believe that actually worked," said Deanna. "I mean, we just walked right out the front door."

Hammer gave her one of his rare smiles. "Loki really thinks I'm stupid."

Graham chimed in, "We're free. I can't thank you enough for that, Hammer. But what do we do now? Lock is likely to have people out looking for us. They are probably already watching our families."

Hammer nodded. Graham was probably right. Loki was probably already trying to hunt them down. Currently, they were holed up in an old abandoned building that the city owned. Graham knew about it, and had offered it as a place to catch their breath after escaping Key Tower.

Hammer had turned only once and stared upon the great building. It was huge. Of course it was, thought Hammer; Loki would of course build a giant building.

His thoughts were interrupted by a young officer. "So going home is pretty much out of the question?"

"Yes," said Graham. "I'm afraid that any of us try to go home, we'll just be recaptured. The entire city is against us."

"So do we run? Do we just take off and try to get as far away as possible?" asked the young officer.

There were murmurs through the large group. Hammer didn't bother counting, but figured there were about thirty people with them, between the captives and the guards he had persuaded to lead them out. There was discontent all around. They were all scared. They all wanted to go home, but that wasn't a realistic option.

As the crowd started to get upset, Hammer stepped forward. His powerful voice boomed out, getting everyone's attention. "Enough!"

The crowd got instantly silent. They had all seen him in action, and no one wanted to anger the giant man with the red beard. He glared at all of them intently.

"We aren't going to argue like children. It's pointless. Our situation is very simple. We can't go home while Lock is looking for us. If we run, we leave our families and everything we care about behind. For those of you who want that option, I won't try to stop you, but I will tell you this. As long as I draw breath, I shall oppose Lock and his Ragnarok Begins. I will be taking the fight to him. I will ensure that his evil little reign comes to an end. I will fight them. I will fight for your country which his gang is overrunning. I will fight for your families, which now must live in fear of his wrath. I will fight to defeat the fear he has over you. And hear me clearly: I will win. I will defeat Lock. I will bring his minions and his tower to the ground. I welcome any of you to stand with me, but I understand if his power over you has driven you to cowardice. Any who wishes to leave may do so, but any who wishes to stay may stand and fight with me. You will be on the front lines when the greatest threat to your world is defeated. It is your choice. Make it quickly."

Much to Hammer's surprise, everyone chose to stay.

GRAHAM KNEW OF a house where they could hole up outside of town. It belonged to the officer that had betrayed him and caused him to wind up in Loki's hands. What made it even better was that the officer had a pretty decent gun collection. With food, guns, and an actual house at their disposal, the entire group felt better about their situation. They also found a large amount of cash in the gun safe. Deanna had come up with the idea of sending a few people to a store for additional food, walkie-talkies, and pre-paid cell phones.

Deanna was convinced that she still had contacts within the media that would be willing to help them. She had been given full access to the home computer and one of the phones, under Hammer's strict instructions to do nothing that could be traced back to the house. Graham had also started contacting the few people he still knew that could be trusted. He knew something about Lock's weapon supply chain; that was what got him locked up in the first place. Graham used his contacts to determine that Lock was still moving weapons into Little Rock by the truckload. In a matter of hours they had a plan for their first attack.

IT WAS THE kind of truck that people rented when they were moving. Hammer didn't recognize the company name, but it was right on time. There were two cars in front of it and two cars behind that were obviously escorts. This had also been known to them beforehand. The truck and its escorts were waiting at a red light.

Hammer signaled for his men to move forward. As soon as the light turned green, the vehicles started moving. As the truck started rolling forward a pickup truck pulled out in front of it, causing the truck to slam its breaks and lightly hit the pickup.

The pickup truck driver stepped out in the street and started apologizing to the driver of the moving truck. The moving truck driver started yelling for him to move his pickup. The pickup driver was insisting on trading insurance. Hammer smiled; the plan was going perfect so far.

The escorts started getting out of their vehicles. There were close to twenty men. It was more than they had planned for, but Hammer wasn't calling off the plan. He signaled the rest of his men.

Snipers wielding deer rifles began shooting at the escorts. Hammer, Graham, and several other men charged toward the moving truck wielding shotguns and pistols.

The Ragnarok Begins gang members opened fire with their automatics, but they were still looking for the snipers above them. Hammer and his team started dropping them quickly. The gang members were better equipped, but Hammer and company's surprise attack completely overwhelmed them.

The driver of the moving truck threw it into reverse and slammed into the front of the escort car behind him. He put the truck in drive and began pulling forward.

Before anyone could say anything, Hammer was already moving. He dropped his assault rifle and dove onto the back of the truck. He hung on for dear life as the truck started building speed. He could hear his men yelling from behind him, while they continued the gunfight in the street.

Hammer pulled himself up on top of the truck. He inched his way across the roof until he was near the cab. He had to move quickly. If the driver or passenger realized he was up there, then all they needed to do was slam the brakes and he would be sent flying.

Once he got himself in place, he leaned over the side and punched right through the passenger window straight into the passenger's face. He pulled the passenger out through the window and let him fall to the street. Then he threw himself into the passenger's seat.

The driver looked at him in shock and horror. Hammer presented his 1911 and said, "Why don't you go ahead and stop the truck?"

The driver complied.

A few minutes later, Hammer pulled the truck up to the spot where his team was supposed to meet after the heist. Graham and the others ran forward to meet him. They lifted the back door of the truck and discovered that they had recovered numerous crates of assault rifles, ammo, and grenades. It was well beyond what their small group needed.

"You know," said Graham. "I'm starting to think you might not be making this whole Thor thing up after all."

Hammer smiled and they headed for the safe house. When they arrived, Deanna beckoned him to the computer. Displayed on the screen was a local news site. Across the front of the page it said, "Join the resistance! Fight back today! Stop Ragnarok Begins! Reports say this might truly be a mythological war between the Norse gods! Could the criminal mastermind Lock truly be Loki? Could the hero arising to face him truly be Thor, the Protector of Man?"

Hammer looked at her incredulously. "How?"

She laughed. "I'm a reporter. These days, having a trusted hacker is almost a requirement. Half the city has seen this; in a few hours, maybe half the country."

Hammer was impressed. "I hadn't even thought about computers."

Deanna laughed, "Look, I'm not someone for using a gun,

but I can help you guys in my own way. I can get the word out."

"If you think it will help," he said, though he wasn't truly convinced.

"Don't worry, Thor," she winked. "I have a few tricks up my sleeve."

THE PLAN WAS a guerilla strike on the club where many of Loki's top men hung out. Over the last few weeks, every attack they made went perfectly well. Loki was being more careful and was searching for them everywhere. They were gaining allies, though. They had heard rumors of groups in the streets attacking Ragnarok Begins all over the city. It wasn't just in Little Rock, though. Deanna said that attacks were beginning all over the country. They were making a dent, and Loki knew it. The best part was that the people were rallying in the name of Thor. It didn't mean that people believed in him again, but they believed in the idea. Hammer knew it was time to step up their game. As well as things had been going, he knew that taking down some of Loki's top lieutenants would make a huge impact.

The plan failed miserably. Loki's men continued their business as usual, but they had acquired more bodies. They were expecting an attack on the club. They wanted Hammer's group to attack them there.

Now his force was scattered and slowly being overrun. Hammer, Graham, and around ten others had been forced back to an old abandoned warehouse. They were getting closed off. He didn't know where the rest of his team was. They had lost communication. As the minutes wore on, his numbers were dwindling, while more of Loki's men were gathering. They were severely outnumbered.

Hammer led his remaining men toward the roof of the

warehouse. The walls were being ripped to shreds by gunfire. He knew that the enemy forces would be in the warehouse before they could do anything about it.

The roof was clear, but he could hear helicopters in the distance. Below them the building was completely surrounded by both Ragnarok Begins and police. They were working together.

"So he's not even hiding that he owns the force now," said Graham bitterly.

Hammer looked around him. "Graham, I need you to get these guys out of here."

Graham looked at him. "I'd be happy to, but I don't see any options."

"I'm going to give you an opportunity," said Hammer, "It's me that Loki really wants. I'm willing to bet that his men know it, too."

"So what?" asked Graham. "You're going to turn yourself over to them?"

"Of course not," said Hammer. "I'm going to fight them."

"You can't fight them alone," Graham yelled.

"Of course I can," said Hammer. "Haven't you been paying attention? I'm the frickin' God of Thunder!"

Hammer turned, ran across the roof, and jumped, clearing the next roof with ease. He spun around and as the helicopter started closing in, he opened fire. The helicopter moved toward him. He pointed his gun to the street and opened fire on the police and Ragnarok Begins gangsters.

With all of the attention focused on him, he jumped across to another roof. He wasn't sure that they would send everyone at him, but it was the only opportunity he saw to try to get his team out safely.

The helicopter closed in and a man using a mounted

machine gun opened fire. Hammer ran on, pushing with everything he had. He dove behind an air conditioning unit. Bullets punched through the metal around his head. It wasn't going to protect him for long.

He was trapped, but suddenly they weren't firing at him anymore. He could still hear the machine gun cracking off shots, though. He moved his head around to the outside and saw that Graham and his allies were shooting at the helicopter. The machine gunner had turned and was shooting at them.

Hammer charged toward the helicopter. When he came to the edge of the roof he jumped with every bit of strength he had. He cleared the space between himself and the helicopter and smashed into the back of the machine gunner.

Hammer clambered to his feet and pushed the man out of the helicopter. He grabbed the machine gun in one hand and pointed his pistol at the man in the cockpit. He screamed, "Keep this thing in the air if you want to live! Circle around to where your buddies are!"

Hammer had never used a gun like this, but he could tell where the trigger was. As they came over top of the cops and Ragnarok Begins, he pulled the trigger. Rounds burst from the gun, tearing everything in its path to pieces. His attack caused total panic in the streets.

Two other helicopters were moving in. He opened fire on them, and they returned the favor. Bullets ripped around him, but he continued firing. He spotted the center of the enemy force and ordered the helicopter pilot to fly over.

With the constant impact of bullets, he knew that the helicopter was taking too much damage, and that it was inevitably going down. The god of thunder accepted this fact, and decided to take as many enemies with him as he could.

He opened fire on one of the opposing helicopters again,

and it began spinning out of control. It hit the ground in a ball of fire and twisted metal. His own pilot was screaming something at him, but he ignored it and opened fire on the other helicopter. His ride was getting rougher, and he began to hear sensors going off. His helicopter was about to go down, as well. He ignored it and focused on the helicopter attacking them.

Somehow he managed to get the killshot in just before his own helicopter began spinning out of control. As it started spiraling downward, he pointed the gun at the ground and the blurred images of enemies swirling by and getting closer as he fell. He opened fire. There was no way he could tell if he was hitting anything.

As the ground grew close, he let go of the gun and dove out the door. His body hit the pavement with a sickening thud and he could feel the helicopter smashing the ground right behind him. Flames and heat licked his back, and he screamed. He was done. There was no way he could have survived the crash.

He glanced around him. Somehow he was still alive, and men were racing toward his body. He staggered to his feet and smashed into the first-charging man. He threw him to the ground and hefted his gun. He slung it to his shoulder and began firing at the other men charging him. He dropped them all.

Through the smoke and debris he could see the traitor Sam peering at him and barking orders. Hammer charged toward him, and realized that he was only feeling minor pain. How could he be only experiencing minor pain after a helicopter crash?

Sam saw him coming and raised his gun. Hammer dove behind a forgotten cop car as the bullets flew over his head. He took only a moment to view his surroundings. The three helicopter crashes along with the damage caused by his machine gun had caused momentary panic in the streets. But Loki's men were now working their way toward him again.

He didn't have much time. Screaming a warcry from the old days, he jumped straight over the top of the cop car and began firing his gun while he was still in the air. The two enemies around Sam fell. Hammer's feet hit the ground at a dead run and he charged at Sam. Sam took cover behind a car, and without thinking about it, Hammer shouldered the car with all of his might. The car slid away from him, putting Sam out in the open.

Sam stood before him in horror. "How? How did you do that?"

Hammer strolled calmly toward him.

"It's true, isn't it?" asked Sam hysterically. "You really are Thor?"

Sam raised his pistol in a shaking hand. Before he could fire, Hammer was on him and grabbed the gun from his hand. He raised it up for all to see and crushed it between his fingers.

Sam screamed and charged him with a knife. Hammer's own gun thundered in his hand. Sam stopped running and looked down at the hole in his stomach. He fell to his knees and clutched the wound.

"Wouldn't you like to know?" Hammer answered the dying man, then facing the crowd he roared, "Who's next? Who else dares challenge the God of Thunder?"

Lightning flashed in his eyes as he spoke. He still didn't have his full power, but some had returned to him. People obviously believed again.

No one challenged. Hammer turned and walked away.

"AS THIS WAR prepares to enter its final stage, which

side are you on? Do you choose the side of the criminal Lock? Or do you choose the side of Hammer, the man opposing Lock? Do you believe that these two men are actually gods from Asgard? Well folks, I'm Deanna Carrie, and I for one believe that is exactly the truth. I've seen what these men can do, and personally, I believe that the man named Hammer is none other than Thor himself. I believe that if you want freedom that you should choose to side with him as he prepares his final battle against his arch-nemesis Loki."

Hammer ignored the recording and turned to the woman herself. "I don't know if this should go out."

She shrugged. "Too late. It's already out there. It's being broadcast on every major news channel in the country."

"So Loki knows exactly when we plan to strike?" asked Graham. "Guys, I think that's a really bad idea."

Hammer shrugged. "I guess it's too late now. Maybe some people will actually show up to join us."

AS HAMMER'S GROUP entered the long street that led to Key Tower, they were suddenly surrounded by people stepping out of buildings and approaching them. His men started drawing their weapons, but Hammer put up his hand.

"I don't think these are Loki's men."

A random man approached. "Thor! Is that you?"

Hammer eyed the man suspiciously. "I guess that depends on who's asking."

The man smiled. "A volunteer! I saw you on the news!"

"Is that so?" asked Hammer suspiciously.

"Yeah!" said the man brightly, and turned to the others. "We all did! There are tons of people. We want to join for your last battle against Loki! We want that sumbitch out of our town!"

"All right then," said Hammer. "You're welcome to come along."

As they continued marching down the street, more and more people started gathering around them. His original group of twenty became fifty, then one hundred, two hundred, five hundred, a thousand. There were so many people joining them that Hammer couldn't even estimate. As he looked back down the street there were armed citizens are far as he could see.

"Wow," said Graham. "She did it, Hammer. She built us an army."

Hammer nodded. "Let's just hope it's enough."

As they came into range of Key Tower, they realized that the entire block surrounding the tower had been turned into a killing ground. Numerous helicopters swirled above them. Hundreds upon hundreds of Loki's men had the streets blocked with vehicles. Hammer could only assume that every floor of the tall buildings around them were also full of Loki's soldiers.

This last ditch full-on assault was suicide. He had thousands of human lives at his back, but there were equally as many in front of him. Loki had pulled together his entire force. If they tried to charge, these people were going to be killed in droves. What could he do, though? His powers were coming back quickly now, but he still wasn't sure exactly how strong he was.

There was only one thing that he knew to do. He turned to Graham. "It's been an honor fighting beside you, Chief."

"You too, Thor," said Graham.

"It's just Hammer."

"No, it's not son." Graham smiled at him. "Today you are Thor again. Today you are going to earn back the mantle you lost. You are going to become the Protector of Man once again."

Hammer nodded. "Okay, have everyone stay well behind

my charge, but move in as soon as it's clear."

"Wait," said Graham. "What are you planning to do?"

"I'm going to find out if you're right." Thor smiled and turned toward the enemy line.

He charged. His speed was so great that he was little more than a blur. The enemy couldn't line up shots and suddenly he was amongst them. He smashed straight through the first row of their car barriers. His strength was far beyond human. He hadn't felt this way for so long, but it felt natural, easy.

He grabbed a car and hurled it through the air. He grabbed another and did the same. Gunfire rang out all around him, but nothing hit him. He was too quick. He turned the defensive lines of Ragnarok Begins into mush. Men screamed and ran at him. A helicopter swept in and tried to open fire, but he pelted it with a mini-van. The helicopter exploded out of sight.

He glanced back to see Graham leading a charge into the confused and scattered enemy line. They fell away as the tidal wave of angry citizens fell upon them. Thor smiled, and continued his charge. He ripped a path of havoc through the lines of Ragnarok Begins, and they all started falling back.

He ran toward Key Tower. His allies were still moving up behind him. They had a clear shot at the building now. There were still maybe thousands of enemies, but most were retreating. He knew that Graham could handle the ground battle from here. He did need to do something about the air support, though. The helicopters would eat the humans alive.

It would take too long to try to peg them all with cars. Loki was a slippery devil, and even if his powers were returning, too, he might simply try to escape. Thor knew he had to get to him.

Suddenly he had an idea that would serve a dual purpose. He ran towards a low-flying helicopter. When he was close enough, he used his inhuman strength to jump into the air and grab on. He flipped the bird at the nearest helicopter, which returned fire. He swung himself through the air and landed on the firing helicopter as it destroyed the first. The machine gunner tried to turn the gun on him, but he yanked him from his position and sent him out for flying lessons.

Quickly, he pointed the gun at the two other nearest helicopters. He dropped both of them. He roared for the pilot to take him to the top of the tower. As they came to the top he could see Loki standing on the roof watching him. He grabbed the pilot's stick and forced the helicopter toward Loki. As he had done before, he bailed out just before the crash. He came up to his feet and found himself facing an unharmed Loki.

Loki smiled. "So nice having powers back, isn't it?"

Thor glared at him.

"It was a nice gesture of your reporter friend to make the world believe in us again, but as usual you weren't smart enough to make sure that she got them to believe in just you."

Thor roared and charged at Loki.

Loki disappeared, and Thor felt a sudden kick to the back of the head. He fell forward and Loki reappeared in front of him to land a solid upper cut to his jaw. Thor swung at him as he fell backwards, but Loki was gone again.

Loki didn't reappear but his voice did. "Having fun yet, nephew? I see that you are still all power and no brains. Pity."

A kick came toward the back of his head again, but Thor heard the displacement of air and spun at the last moment. He grabbed Loki by the foot and swung him around to smash his body into a large air conditioning unit.

Loki was stunned and Thor dove for him, but when he hit the ground there was nothing there. Loki reappeared, doing a quick dance number on Thor's back before Thor could get to his feet. Loki hammered another kick into his head.

Thor was getting frustrated now, but tried to keep his head. If he allowed his emotions to override his thoughts, then Loki would win. He paused again as he did before, and listened. This time Loki tried to take his surprise attack low to the back of Thor's knee cap. Thor spun and kicked Loki in the face. He went down with a thud.

He quickly came back up smiling. "Do you really think that you can beat me, Thor?"

Thor roared his defiance.

Loki laughed. "Indeed, but we can battle this way all day and prove nothing. I think it's time to up the odds."

Loki snapped his fingers, and suddenly two helicopters ascended, one on each side of the roof.

"We're going to play a game, you and me!" Loki declared. "Let's see if you can truly defeat me, nephew! Look at the helicopter over there!"

Thor turned and saw that the door of the helicopter open to display a large cylindrical device just barely big enough to fit inside the helicopter. Wires protruded from various apparati and a blank screen sat on the front.

"Is that a bomb?" asked Thor.

"Not just any bomb," Loki giggled. "That is a nuclear bomb with enough power to send this entire city up in smoke."

Thor turned back toward him, but he was gone. Thor glanced at the other helicopter. Loki was sitting in it now and gave him a little wave. Despite being on the other side of the roof, Thor could still hear him clearly.

"And on this side you have me."

"What's your game, Loki?" Thor asked angrily.

"It's called: let's see what Thor cares about the most!" Loki laughed and held up a small metal device. "You have a choice to make, nephew! It's simple! When I press this button you will have approximately five seconds to get to the bomb and press the big red stop button. If you do, then the bomb will be defused. However, in that five seconds I will be flying away. However, if you choose to come after me, and the bomb passes its five second mark, then a new countdown will start: a ten minute countdown to the end of this city and every living creature in it. And once the countdown starts, there is absolutely no way to stop it. Do you understand?"

Thor just stared at him.

Loki laughed. "It's like this... What do you care about more? Getting the revenge you've desperately wanted all these countless years? Or protecting humanity? Which is it going to be? Personally, I just can't wait to find out."

Loki pressed the button.

Time froze for Thor as he considered his options. It took less than a millisecond to realize that there were no options. He had waited for this opportunity to get his revenge for well over a thousand years. What were a few more?

Thor, the Protector of Man, chose to disarm the bomb.

As soon as he pressed the stop button, he glanced back to where Loki's helicopter was starting to fly away. Suddenly, a lightning bolt from the sky struck the helicopter and it fell. Loki dove out and landed on the roof as the helicopter crashed into the building.

He looked at Thor in horror. "How did you do that?"

"It wasn't me." Thor shrugged. "Bad karma, maybe?"

Before Loki could respond, another voice said, "It was me."

Thor and Loki both turned as a new figure appeared before them. He appeared to be an elderly man, but didn't look the least bit frail. His gray hair hung to his shoulders, and over one eye he wore a silver eye patch.

Thor cried, "Father!"

Odin turned and looked at his son. "The All Father to be exact."

Loki sighed. "Ah, balls."

Thor said, "I don't understand. I thought Loki killed you?"

Odin smiled. "There's a lot that neither of you seems to understand, but today, my son, you've made the first step."

Thor asked, "What do you mean?"

Odin smiled. "Thor, of all of the things that you have been in your life, the Protector of Man is by far the most important. Yet, you chose for so long to ignore it."

Thor bowed his head. "Yes, father. I have failed."

"Yet today you did not," said Odin. "I've been waiting for you to figure that out on your own."

"Why?" asked Thor.

Odin shrugged. "You've always been too headstrong to simply tell. You always must be shown. Besides that, watching you two clowns was rather entertaining. Which reminds me, I've been holding something for you."

Thor's hammer appeared in Odin's hand. He tossed it to him lightly, and Thor caught it smiling. The weight felt good in his hand. It felt right. He turned toward Loki.

"Ah, double balls," cried Loki. "I don't guess you would believe me if I told you that my whole plan all along was to get you to start protecting humanity, as well. I mean it was so important to me that I actually had to fool you into thinking that I was trying to take over the world. So yay team! We did it! High five, Odin! No? Okay. So I'm thinking that we all just go to the bar now to celebrate! What'd ya say nephew?"

Thor answered with his hammer, smashing it into Loki's face. Before Loki could fight back, Thor pelted him several more times until he didn't move.

Odin smiled at him. "I'm proud of you, son."

"Thank you, Father," said Thor.

"All Father," reminded Odin.

Thor smiled. "What should I do with him?"

"I'll take him with me," said Odin.

"He won't be a threat?" asked Thor.

"Nah," replied Odin. "He'll be locked away real nice where he's going. I might even get him a shrink. He is my adopted brother after all."

Thor nodded. "I'll be here, I guess, cleaning up his mess."

Odin smiled. "As you should be... Protector of Man."

The Athena Palladium

Joel Jenkins

ON THE SEVENTH day, the Trojan prophet Helenus broke beneath the tortures of Odysseus, and his loosened tongue spilled the secrets of the gods.

Helenus hung upside down from an acacia tree, and Odysseus slammed scarred knuckles into the prophet's ribs and heard them splinter beneath the blow. "Tell me how to breach the walls of Troy or I'll pound every bone of your body into powder."

Helenus choked up blood and then managed to gargle out a response. "The city of Troy will never fall..."

Odysseus drew back his fist to administer further punishment, but his blow was checked by Helenus's further words.

"...unless three conditions are met."

"We're listening," said Odysseus. "Check thy words that thou speakest only truth!"

"The bones of Pelops must be recovered from Pisa and brought to Trojan shores, and Neoptolemus—the son of Achilles--must brought to battle."

Diomedes watched the proceedings from a nearby boulder, where he chewed on a pomegranate, the braids of his long hair falling about his broad shoulders. "If Neoptolemus is as thick-skulled as his father, it will be no easy task to persuade him."

Odysseus couldn't help but agree, but made no comment. Instead, he addressed the dangling prophet. "You haven't told us the third condition, prophet. Don't cease speaking now, or I shall have to administer some more punishment."

"Please, no," coughed Helenus. "The third condition is that as long as the Palladium of Athena stands inside the walls of Troy, the city shall never fall."

Odysseus examined his bloodied knuckles. "I see. So you give us two nigh-on impossible tasks, and then divulge a third task which is beyond impossible."

"So speak the gods," said Helenus.

Odysseus glanced at Diomedes, who shrugged. "A prophet wouldn't dare lie in the name of the gods. I think you've finally beaten the truth from him."

Odysseus drew out a long knife, which had formerly belonged to Achilles, and ran his thumb across the blade, checking the knife's sharpness. "If you say so, then I suppose we no longer have need of Helenus."

Helenus did not fail to notice the knife in Odysseus's hand. "Please, show me mercy. I have been defeated by Deiphobus, beaten by Odysseus, and now I have betrayed the people of Troy. Is that not punishment enough?"

"You were defeated by Deiphobus because you had the temerity to desire Helen—who is the rightful wife of Menalaus. Neither you, Deiphobus, or Paris—may he rot in Hades—have the right to touch her."

"In his defense," said Diomedes, "Helen has bewitched many a man. Thousands have died since Paris stole her away. So, in a way, have we not all been swayed by the spell of her beauty?"

Odysseus contemplated the knife. "So, Helenus, Diomedes

has seen that you have been exonerated on one count, but the beating you received from me is something due anyone foolish enough to abandon the safety of Troy."

"I could not stand to see Helen betrothed to Deiphobus," gasped Helenus, his face screwed into an expression of excruciating pain.

"I would exonerate him on that point, also," mused Diomedes as he spat out pomegranate seeds. "Is not that the reason that we Greeks are hounding the gates of Troy—because we cannot stand the thought of a filthy Trojan laying their hands upon our fair Helen?"

"A fair enough point," agreed Odysseus, "if one ignores the fact that Helenus, himself, is a filthy Trojan."

"Let's ignore that petty point for the moment," said Diomedes. "After all, a man cannot be faulted for his heritage, since he cannot choose it. What about the third reason that Helenus gave in his request for leniency?"

"Ah," sighed Odysseus, "that we should show mercy, because he betrayed his people. I admit that I don't find the argument very compelling. You may not be able to choose your own blood, but you can choose whether or not to betray it."

"But I was compelled!" protested Helenus, his breath coming in ragged gasps.

"So you were," said Odysseus, "but I find that no excuse."

"Please! I beg mercy of you!" cried Helenus.

Odysseus drew the blade across Helenus's throat. "I never promised mercy, prophet."

As Helenus's dark blook soaked the ground, Odysseus turned to Diomedes and began to wipe clean the knife with which he had slain the Trojan prophet. "So where do we start, Diomedes. If we are to bring this long war to a close, should we not do it in a way that heaps glory and honor upon ourselves?"

"Naturally," agreed Diomedes. "I am inclined to assay the most difficult task first. If we cannot remove Athena's image from Troy, then there is no point attempting to enlist Neoptolemus or stealing the bones of Pelops."

"Agreed," said Odysseus, who sheathed his knife.

"But how to breach the walls of Troy? Even on a moonless night the walls are brightly lit with a thousand torches."

Odysseus shook back his brown hair, and his green eyes glinted with savage light. "Last night Achilles came to me in a dream and showed me the location of a muddy culvert that burrowed beneath the city walls."

Diomedes green eyes showed skepticism. "And does this culvert actually exist?"

"You think that Achilles would appear so that he could mislead me?"

Diomedes shrugged his broad shoulders. "We are speaking of Achilles, aren't we? A man whose pride and vanity kept him from joining arms with us when we needed him most? Maybe he's angry that you bear his arms and wear his armor, and wants you to join him in death."

"Nay," said Odysseus. "It was the hand of Athena that helped me defeat Ajax and win Achilles' spoils. I tell you, this is a dream sent from Athena. She wants us to steal the palladium. Of this I am certain!"

"I am certain of nothing, except that I would like to return to the bed of my wife, Aegialeia. The glories and honors of bloodshed and battle are wearing thin."

"So you would shirk your duty and give away the honor and glory of accomplishing such an astounding feat?"

Diomedes chuckled. "No. I have to admit that the idea of stealing the holy image of Athena out from under the noses of the Trojans is one that appeals to me. And if it gets me home to

Aegialeia faster, then all the better."

"Meet me just before dusk," said Odysseus. "And bring a third man who is good with a spear—but no more. If we approach the wall in too large of numbers we will be sure to be discovered."

"I'll speak with Mineus. He makes a fine spear cast and is anxious to make a name for himself."

"As should any Greek warrior," said Odysseus. "We'll find that culvert and make our way to the temple of Athena."

Diomedes rose and stretched his muscular frame. "I'll tell Mineus not to get his hopes up. There's no reason to disappoint him, should we not find this secret culvert that Achilles revealed to you in your dream."

Odysseus grinned. "It will be there. I tell you, Athena sent Achilles to show me the way so that when Helenus divulged his prophecies we would know how to accomplish the tasks set before us."

"Time will tell," said Diomedes, "but it seems to me that the guidance of the gods is fickle. Mayhap Achilles was sent to you by Ares to lie and lead you to your doom."

THE SUN SANK low over the wine-dark oceans as Odysseus, Diomedes, and Mineus gathered for their venture. They dressed in rags, like beggars, their torn cloaks concealing the sword blades girded at their waists. They crept through the brush, leaving behind the vast encampments of the Greeks that spread along the seashores, the palisades built from the carcasses of their ships, and the vast fleets that rode the glistering swells at their barnacled anchors.

Like ghosts, they disappeared into the green-capped hills that surrounded the impregnable walls of Troy. Blood had drenched these hills and the life-giving ichor had fertilized the verdant swards even in the deaths of many, both Trojan and Greek.

Mineus was sharp-eyed and lithe and had no difficulty keeping up with the hawk-nosed Odysseus, whose intensity burned as hot as the Agean sun, or the mild-mannered Diomedes, who no one observing would suspect of the temerity or iron intestines to face and challenge both Ares and Aphrodite and send them fleeing from the field of battle.

Mineus scrambled up the rocky shale that grew thick with prickly shrubs. "Just how do you propose to breach the walls of the Trojan curs?"

Odysseus scrutinized the landscape. "I'm looking for a split tree that has been sundered by a javelin throw, and the tree has grown up around it."

"When did you see it last?" asked Mineus.

"Last night in a dream," said Odysseus. "Achilles showed it to me—said that the sign of the javelin-become-tree would show me the way through the walls of Troy."

Mineus knew full well that only the shade of Achilles could speak with Odysseus, for he had been slain in the field of battle by Paris, struck by an arrow in the heel—the only part of Achilles which was not impervious. "The gods want us to defeat the Trojans, else they would not have sent Achilles to provide omens and auguries."

Diomedes spoke in wry tones. "Only some of the gods pine for our victory. There are many others that are pitted against us. We are but pawns in a duel between the gods, and the world is their gameboard."

"But has not Athena herself aided you?" objected Mineus.

"Perhaps she has guided my spear thrust or throw," said Diomedes, "but the favors of the gods change with the winds, and finding the favor of one may find you in the disfavor of another."

They crested a hilltop and Odysseus cried out in victory. "I see the tree!"

Indeed, following the trajectory of Odysseus's fingertip, they could see a cypress tree which grew up around the shaft of a javelin. Odysseus went to the javelin and taking hold of the shaft, he wrenched it from the cypress which split asunder. Betwixt the roots a gap was revealed which sank into the earth. "Ho," proclaimed Odysseus. "What have we here? Perhaps my dream was sent of Athena, after all. Eh, Diomedes?"

"It's a hole in the earth," admitted Diomedes. "But is it a passage into Troy?"

Odysseus began to climb into the hole. "There's one way to find out, doubter. Now, be quick on my heels, or I shall storm the temple of Athena myself and you'll have no share of the glory and laurels that will be heaped upon my head."

Though skeptical of the source of the dream, Diomedes was no shirker, and he, like Mineus, lacked no boldness, so they slipped into the bosom of the moist earth. Finding themselves at the bottom of a pit, they followed a passage a few steps to the south and discovered a deep trench, trickling with storm water. The trench was not visible from above because of the thick screen of foliage which had completely over-arched the ditch. The blue Aegean sky was blocked from view and the occasional spear of sunlight thrust itself through the brambles, illuminating their splashing steps.

After a time, they were forced to unsheath their swords and use them to hack their way through the brambles and vines so they could ascend the trench, which drew them up close to the walls of Troy.

As they came to the base of the towering walls the voices of the guards upon the wall filtered down to them, and they could catch glimpses of pauldrons and helms that glinted redly in the rays of the falling sun.

"Now do you believe that my dream was from the gods?" whispered Odysseus.

Diomedes put a finger to his lips and pulled aside dangling vines to find that entrance to the city was blocked by rusting iron bars set in a firmament of mortar.

Mineus's excitement at breaching the walls turned to disappointment. "We can't hope to reach the temple of Athena now."

Don't be so ready to accept defeat," said Diomedes. He crossed to the bars and seized hold of them. He put one foot against the bar while he pulled with all his might. The bar creaked and groaned, and then gave way beneath the strength of Diomedes's mighty thews.

On the wall above they heard a voice call out. "Hark, what was that noise?"

Within the trench, Mineus was not slow to respond. He mimicked the sound of a tree frog, which had a similar groaning timbre to its voice as the bending bar.

"It's a frog, you imbecile. A frog that's getting an early start on its evening of carousing."

Diomedes had forced a large enough gap between the bars that he, with his broad shoulders, and Odysseus, with his barrel chest, were narrowly able to scrape through. Mineus was of a more slender build, and even while the guards overhead reverted to their bawdy jests, he slipped easily into the arched storm drain that plumbed beneath the great walls of Troy.

They passed deep into the tunnel's gloom before Odysseus paused and drew out a tar-soaked torch which he ignited with a flint. It blazed into life, illuminating the web-thick corners of the drainage tunnel. Salamanders scuttled for cover and fist-sized spiders retreated into the shadowed corners of their webs.

Mineus eyed the crumbling mortar of the bricks that shored up the tunnel. "When do you think this was built?"

Diomedes struck out with his dagger, lancing a large spider which crept uncomfortably close. "Before the foundations of Troy was laid, and long since forgotten by all but the gods."

"Where do we go?" asked Mineus.

Odysseus thrust out his torch. "We've got two choices, Mineus: forward or backward—and since we don't yet have our hands upon the palladium, it's forward we go."

Already, Diomedes was moving through the tunnel, using his sword blade to cut down viscous strands of webbing that ensnared both insect and salamander, bodies withered and dessicated—sucked dry by avaricious arachnids.

They plunged through the shadows for some time, only coming to a halt when the drainage tunnel split into two corridors. Of these, only the corridor on the right hand was large enough to let them pass upright. The other shrank to such a size that they would be forced to crawl.

"Assay the passage on the right," said Odysseus. "If we find ourselves at an impasse we'll return to the smaller passage."

This sounded reasonable to Diomedes and he began to ascend the passage to the right, Odysseus taking the position behind him, followed by the intrepid Mineus, who produced a short javelin from beneath his cloak.

The sound of dripping water echoed in the confines of the tunnel, coming to their ears as reflected by a hundred arching surfaces. Ahead, a shaft of sunlight shone through a drain grating, illuminating the darkness. As they drew closer, Odysseus thrust the tip of his torch into the waters through which they tread, extinguishing the flame, and they traveled the last fifty cubits guided by that shaft of sunlight.

The Athena Palladium

Diomedes was tall enough to reach the grating and he listened carefully, finally taking a chance and pushing the heavy grating upward and heaving it off to the side where it lay on the cobblestones of the street. Again, Diomedes and Odysseus barely fit through the open shaft, but they emerged in a sloping back alley of Troy. Mineus was the last to emerge and he dragged the grating back into place, and they stood in their beggar's rags inside the great City of Troy, within the high walls that had so long thwarted the efforts of the Greeks.

They cast their eyes about and saw the temple of Athena on the hilltop to their right. Odysseus jabbed his finger in the direction of the gleaming spires. "There's our destination, brothers, and the glory is ours to seize."

"An honorable return home to my Aegieliea will be sufficient for me," said Diomedes.

Mineus concealed his javelin beneath his ragged, mud-soiled robe. "As for me, I'd like a place on the councils and spoils and concubines enough to richly appoint my manse when I return."

"If we succeed, all that and more will be yours," promised Odysseus.

"Be careful that you take nothing from the temple of Athena but the palladium," warned Diomedes. "The honor of hosting the palladium is to be sought after, but Athena will not turn a blind eye to the wholesale pillaging of her temple."

Mineus nodded, but clearly his mind was elsewhere.

One by one they emerged from the alley, their weapons hidden beneath the soiled rags of their robes. Their hearts were in their throats as they came to view the citizens of Troy: dark-tressed and deep-bosomed women choosing their victuals from the carts of vendors while dirty-faced children tugged at the hems of their skirts, slaves bent under heavy burdens and urged along with freshly-cut switches, soldiers girded in leather harnesses and crimson cloaks, marching to the walls to relieve those on watch. To these last, the trio disguised as beggars feared, they might fall under scrutiny that would reveal that they were not mendicants, but rather soldiers of the enemy Greeks. However, few gave scant scrutiny to the beggars among them, choosing to ignore their existence.

So, it was with greater confidence they began to wend their way through the streets, climbing their way toward Athena's temple.

Diomedes observed the plentiful food and the carts of fruits and vegetables that were being pulled away as dusk began to settle upon Troy. "They live like kings in houses of stone and timber while we live like dogs in leaking tents."

"The women here are beautiful," said Mineus, a wistful note in his voice.

"You think so because you've been without female companionship for the years since we've been besieging Troy," said Odysseus.

"It's high time that we end this war," said Diomedes. "So many have died for just one woman."

"That Helen has been stolen away from her rightful husband is a stain upon Greek honor," said Oddyseus. "If we let this slight pass unavenged, then what other puling nations will think us easy prey?"

"True enough," said Diomedes, "and all more reason to deliver the final blow that will crush Troy."

A tinkling voice fell upon their ears and they saw the fair form of a woman approach through the dusk. She had a hundred soldiers with her, and they guarded her on all sides. "Ho, mendicants. Do you have enough food to fill your bellies this fine evening?"

"Nay," said Diomedes, "our bellies are empty." He recognized the woman now, for her supernal beauty was famed far and near, and he had once vied for her hand in marriage, only to be beaten by Menelaus for the honor. "Helen," he said as she approached.

"You know of me, mendicant?"

"It is your beauty that has launched a thousand ships of war," said Diomedes. "Even the lowliest of beggars knows your name and your face," said Diomedes.

Helen came near to him, surrounded by her coterie of guardians who did not seem amused that the wife of their master, Deiphobus, would hold court with street rabble. Helen handed Diomedes a small loaf of still-warm bread that had been baked in the brick ovens of her husband. Then, in turn, she doled out others to Odysseus and Meneus. "Your voices and aspects seem familiar to me."

"Surely," replied Odysseus, "it is your native kindness that recognizes all as brother and sister and breeds a sense of familiarity with even the lowliest of Troy's people."

"You have an elegant way with words, mendicant," said Helen, and her laugh was like the tinkle of wind chimes. "Surely, you have a silver tongue like Odysseus of Greece."

"I know of no such man," replied Odysseus.

"But the Trojan soldiers know him and fear him," replied Helen, "for he is bold enough to stride even the streets of Troy if he could find away."

"That would be foolhardiness," said Odysseus.

"Indeed, it would be," agreed Helen. "For if Odysseus and his companion-in-arms, the bold Diomedes, ever attempted to steal into the city and carry me back to Greece they would find that my new husband, Deiphobus, has a hundred brave swords defending me night and day."

The chests of Helen's honor guard swelled as they were mentioned and they stood straighter and taller upon hearing those few words fall from her lips.

"And were they to be so foolhardy," said Diomedes, "what would you advise them to do?"

"In no uncertain words I would tell them to take no such action. They should not throw their lives away in such a futile effort against so many brave men. I would that never again a drop of blood be spilt in my name, for already my heart is broken at the carnage that I have caused."

Truly, Diomedes had been considering such a course of action, but three swords against one hundred in the center of Troy did seem the height of recklessness. "May your kindness be returned many times."

"Fare thee well," called Helen.

"She is beautiful," said Mineus in a wistful voice as Helen and her contingent of guards withdrew themselves to go and meet Deiphobus near the walls, leaving the three beggars to continue their climb past rows of heavily-laden olive trees and toward the temple of Athena, the last rays of the setting sun gleaming from the burnished copper surfaces of it domes.

"What's our plan?" asked Mineus as they approached the gates of the temple.

Odysseus grinned. "Just watch Diomedes and I."

"And then what?"

"Follow our lead," said Diomedes.

"And what will be your lead?"

"We like to improvise." Diomedes went to the very gate of Athena's temple and rapped on the gate with a mallet. In a few moments a priest approached the gate. "What do you want, vermin? We have no tolerance for vagrants on our holy grounds."

The Athena Palladium

"Please spare an alm for a trio of poor beggars," said Diomedes, who hunched himself over to disguise his stature.

"We have no coin for the likes of you," said the priest. "Now, make yourselves scarce."

"Then just spare a few crumbs for our hungry bellies," begged Diomedes. "Mayhap you have a crust or two from the bounty of your tables?"

The priest picked up a stick and approached the gate. He raised it over his head and brought it down through the bars of the gate, striking Diomedes on the upraised arm. "I said begone, mendicants!"

The priest attempted to pull the stick back so that he could strike the beggar again, but to his amazement he found that the beggar had caught hold of it and would not relinquish his grip. Instead, the beggar jerked the stick forward and dragged the priest close enough, so that the beggar was able to catch hold of the priest's robes and drag him against the bars of the gate.

"If you'll not share a crust, then we'll take it," said Diomedes. His habitual calm had disappeared and been replaced with a fire that raged in his eyes.

Odysseus moved alongside Diomedes and thrust his sword blade between the bars of the gate and into the side of the priest, who gushed black bile from his bowels and finally ceased his writhing and twitching.

"Hold him fast," barked Odysseus.

"I've got him," spat Diomedes. "I heard the clank of keys beneath his robes."

Odysseus needed no further urging and he tore the robe open, revealing a ring of three keys on a braided belt beneath. He plucked them away and Diomedes tossed the leaking body of the priest back into the courtyard.

"There's a squad of guardsmen climbing the hill," warned

Mineus, who glanced down the twisting, cobbled lane that swayed with the heavy branches of the flanking olive trees.

Odysseus threaded one thick arm through the bars and with some fumbling found the keyhole. The foot treads of the squad grew louder as he tried the first and second keys. The third key slipped into the lock and Odysseus turned it, unlocking the gate so that they were able to push it open and slide through the gap.

Diomedes grasped the dead priest by the torn robes and heaved the body behind a row of palms, while Odysseus shut the gate and locked it.

"Where to now?" asked Mineus.

Diomedes motioned to the shrine of the pillared temple. "Into the holy of holies, my friend. Where else would they keep the personification of Athena on earth?"

They climbed broad steps past gold-plated plinths and granite pillars that supported the jutting veranda. With quick steps, they entered through the arched portal, where the fumes of jasmine and myrrh incense mingled heavy in the air.

Almost immediately they were accosted by crimson-robed priests, who shouted for them to halt, and began to curse them for their sacrilege. When the trio of beggars ignored their cries the priests swept aside the flaps of their robes and revealed short swords that glinted back the ruddy light of the overhanging braziers. The priests descended upon the three Greeks, and for a few moments all was a chaos of flashing blades. Screams echoed in the vast halls of Athena's temple, and blood gushed on the marble floors as swords clanged and flesh was cloven. When the chaos subsided, Diomedes, Odysseus, and Mineus were standing among the strewn bodies of dead and dying priests.

"Six of them," counted Odysseus. "That's two apiece."

Diomedes was sure that he had accounted for at least three of them, but he said nothing. If the last hadn't been distracted by Odysseus he would not have been so easy to kill.

"Into the holy of holies," barked Diomedes. "There's sure to be more of them around."

They continued down the corridors and mounted steps that carried them toward the central dome, past brazen statues which depicted the glorious figure of Athena as imagined by the greatest of Troy's artisans, the mad Theocleise. For a moment they couldn't help but to stop and gaze at the beauty of the work that had been rendered in bronze; the rapture was broken finally by the exigency of their situation, and they knew that they must not linger. At the base of each plinth was a target of beaten gold that was engraved with a prayer to Athena. Diomedes plucked up one of these and hoisted it in front of him.

"I thought you said 'no looting'," spoke Odysseus.

"I'll not leave the temple with the target," replied Diomedes.

Mineus eyed the other target with appeciation and hoisted it with a groan. "I can scarcely lift it, but perhaps I could drag it back to the ships."

"We'll need to move fast once we get our hands on the palladium," said Diomedes, "and we don't want to offend Athena. I'm already in the disfavor of Aphrodite and Ares. Athena is the only goddess that stands between me and punishment by the gods."

Mineus seemed puzzled. "You don't think that slaying six of her priests will bring her enmity?"

"That we should take the palladium of Athena was revealed to me in a dream from the gods," said Odysseus. "We spilled the blood of her priests so that we may obtain the honor of guarding the palladium."

"But whatever you do," warned Diomedes, "do not lay a hand upon her virgin nephanims. Those she guards most zealously."

Again, Mineus's eyes became enraptured, and the thoughts of the virgin nephanims caused him to lay aside the golden target and follow Odysseus and Diomedes up the stair.

Before they could reach the apex of the stairs there was a rush and rustle of robes from above as four priests rushed from the shadows, launching spears at the invading Greeks, who had now abandoned their beggars robes and left them lying at the base of the stairs.

Odysseus hewed the head from one of the spears as it flew toward him, and the point and shaft rebounded harmlessly. Diomedes, who made the largest target, lifted his shield of beaten gold and caught two of the spears. One deflected away and the iron head of the other tore through the shield, and narrowly missed his forearm.

Mineus ducked behind Diomedes, effectively avoiding all of the hurtling spears. Diomedes rushed up the stairs, tearing out the spear and then plunging into the midst of the priests even as they reached for their sword blades. The great shield of gold bowled over two of the priests and Diomedes' thrust his spear through the bowels of a third, pinning him to a great pillar where he writhed. As the fourth priest drew his sword Odysseus came upon him, hacking him down so that he tumbled to the bottom of the steps. Mineus was no less quick upon his feet than Diomedes and he fell on the two downed priests and slew them before they could rise.

With blade dripping the darkest of blood, Mineus rose from his grisly task. "That's ten priests, by my count."

Odysseus's eyes gleamed. "When we tell the tale around the campfire tonight it will be twenty that we slew."

Again, Mineus was puzzled. "So are you saying that there are ten more priests to slay or are you saying that we should exaggerate the odds that we have overcome?"

The Athena Palladium

"Never let the facts stand in the way of a good story." Odysseus tore away the silken curtains that veiled the holy of holies and strode inside, the smoke of incense wafting away as he passed.

Female nephanims in togas that went over one shoulder and fell to their knees shrieked and ran for cover, trembling in the shadowed corners of the sanctum. All were beautiful, chosen for both this pulchritude and their virtue. Only one stood in their way, shielding them from viewing the palladium, which stood between gilded poles over which was stretched a velvet tent. She was fair-haired and green-eyed and stood boldly. "Do not lay a hand upon the palladium!"

"Stand aside, woman, and you will not be harmed," said Odysseus. "I have dreamed a dream that Troy should stand until the palladium comes into the hands of the Greeks. I come with the blessing of Athena."

"The blessing of Athena lies with whoever holds the palladium," retorted the nephanim. "Flee back to your tents, dogs, before the soldiers of Troy find you and slay you like the vomit-licking curs that you are!" She stepped to the side and reached for a silken cord which hung above, and for that moment the palladium was revealed to the eyes of the invading Greeks.

To the eyes of Mineus it was nothing but a twisted limb harvested from an olive tree, but in a glorious blaze of light the true aspect of Athena's form and even face was represented, and the mind-numbingly beautiful work of the mad sculptor Theocleise was swept away as inferior dross—unable to stand the comparison of Athena's supernal beauty.

High in the copper domes of the temple a bell began to toll and the three Greeks realized that they had allowed the nephanim to sound the alarm that would bring the soldiers of Troy running to the temple. Fleet Mineus was to the nephanim's side in but a moment and he struck her a savage blow which brought blood to her lips, and she toppled back even as the bell continued to peel its mournful dirge. Instead of turning to the task of retrieving the palladium he lingered over the nephanim, admiring her beauty. She beat savagely at Mineus's chest, but he did not heed her struggling and tore down the shoulder of her toga.

"Leave her untouched!" ordered Diomedes. "Already you have brought the wrath of Athena down upon yourself for harming one of her chosen handmaidens. Do you wish to see us all destroyed?"

"You bring the palladium back as your prize," said Mineus. "I am bringing this woman back as mine. She'll warm the nights in my cold tent."

"That one will knife you when you sleep," muttered Odysseus, but his eye was fixed on the palladium. He stepped forward as if to stride into the pavilion and take up the image of Athena, but a tapestry moved aside along one wall of the holy of holies and a eunuch—a giant from the hill tribes surrounding Troy—leaped out and launched a spear. Odysseus heard the rustling of cloth and the rasp of a heavy breath and he leaned aside, the cast of the spear slicing a furrow along his deltoid. The spear continued unimpeded in its course and plunged through Mineus's back, the point bursting out just below his rib cage.

Mineus lurched to his feet, leaving the comely nephanim unmolested, but for a spray of his blood that spattered her toga. He took three steps toward the eunuch, lifting his sword blade, but then he pitched forward and laid still, death rattle in his throat, black blood pooling beneath him, the shaft of the spear still projecting from his back.

The eunuch gave a roar of victory and lifted an axe blade – for in addition to being fearsome spearmen the hill tribes were hewers of wood – lunging across the holy of holies toward Diomedes and Odysseus.

The eunuch swung a mighty blow at Odysseus and the Greek raised his sword to meet the stroke. He blocked the axe blade and stopped it inches short of cleaving his skull. The eunuch roared and swatted Odysseus across the side of the face with the back of his fist.

The mighty Odysseus was stunned and reeled away, but before the eunuch could follow up with an axe blow that might end Odysseus's life, Diomedes charged into the towering eunuch with lowered head. With the crown of his skull he struck the eunuch on the sternum, and bone cracked. Even as Diomedes's head impacted he pushed his sword blade through the eunuch's side, gall spilling out over his fist.

Diomedes wrenched the blade and twisted. The legs of the eunuch became unstrung and he tottered and fell even as Diomedes backed away, for the giant crashed down even as a mighty tree, felled by the axes of the hill tribes, might fall.

The tolling of the bell began to die, but the warning had already rung out and soon the soldiers of Troy would ascend to the temple, and like a pack of wolves rend apart any intruders that they found in their midst.

Diomedes stepped into the pavilion and with great temerity took hold of the image of Athena and threw it over his shoulder, just as Mineus might have thrown the comely nephanim over his shoulder and taken her as a spoil of war.

That same nephanim now retreated, cursing them in the name of Athena. "A bane upon you, Greeks!" She spat the name of their homeland as if it were an epithet. "Never will you return to happy home and hearth, and tragedy will beset you at every port!"

She retreated into the side passage through which the eunuch had emerged, and Diomedes let her go. He wiped the blood from his blade upon the garments of the eunuch and called out to Odysseus.

"Art thou still shaken?"

"It was nothing but a tap," growled Odysseus, clearly embarrassed to have been dealt such a stunning blow. "It caught me off guard."

"He's a giant from the hills," said Diomedes. "The Trojans sometimes capture them as children and press them into service as temple guards when they grow."

"I was still dazzled by the beauty of Athena. That's why the giant caught me unready."

"If you've found your feet, we'd best go. It will be just the two of us. I fear that Mineus will not be returning to the ships with us."

"It was the swift retribution of Athena for daring to profane one of her sanctified nephanims."

"That it was," agreed Diomedes. "I suggest we follow the secret corridor she fled through. Otherwise we'll meet more Trojans than we can best."

"A glorious way to die," mused Odysseus, "but more glory will be due to us if we return with the palladium. Let me carry it. I travel swiftly, even with a burden."

"Nay," replied Diomedes. "I plucked her from the holy of holies, and I will bear her back to the ships."

Odysseus scowled. "Then lead the way, brother. Lead the way."

Diomedes descended into the dimly lit corridors and stairs, flickering sconce light intermittently illuminating the way. There was no sign of the nephanim who had fled before them.

The Athena Palladium

Diomedes was sure that once the Trojan soldiers arrived, the other nephanims who had cowered in the corners of the holy of holies would point out the secret door through which they had left.

Once they emerged from the temple and into the city, they would no longer have the advantage of the beggars' robes which had made them invisible to all but Helen's compassionate eye.

Diomedes paused as they passed a niche that contained hooks holding an array of priestly robes. "Put these on. Maybe they'll help us from being recognized."

"Clever enough," said Odysseus and he pulled on the robes. "But how we will disguise the palladium?"

Diomedes tore down a tapestry and wrapped it around the celestial form of the palladium. When they exited from a little-used door at the base of the temple they were attired as priests of Athena, and they moved past squads of warriors that ascended through the olive trees that stood silent sentinel along the winding cobble road.

"Ho, priests!" called a Trojan warrior. "What trouble besets the temple of Athena?"

"The holy of holies has been invaded by Greeks!" answered wily Odysseus. "We narrowly escaped with the palladium and are taking it to sanctuary in the inner city."

The warrior's eyes goggled as if hoping his vision could pierce the drapes that concealed the palladium. "That's the palladium that you're carrying?"

"Aye," said Diomedes. "If we want to retain the favor of Athena we must keep it safe from dirty Greek hands."

"Yes, we must," agreed the warrior, and he urged his squad up the hill. "We'll flay those Greeks alive and throw them mewling over the walls as an example to their brethren."

Diomedes and Odysseus wasted no time reaching the lower

city and finding the alley and grating from which they had sneaked into Troy.

"Give me the palladium and I'll lower her down to you," suggested Odysseus.

Diomedes clambered into the hole. "Nay, I've got a good grip on her." He carefully maneuvered the palladium so that it would follow him down the hole, and he again placed it over his shoulder once his feet were settled firmly in the muck of the drainage tunnel.

Odysseus swung down after Diomedes and splashed into the tunnel. He knew that the greater glory would fall to Diomedes if it was he who bore the palladium of Athena back into camp; this pinprick of jealousy began to work within him, fed by the Goddess Aphrodite, whose anger was exceedingly hot against Diomedes, who had once come nigh unto slaying her when she descended into battle. Diomedes unwrapped a bit of the palladium and let the translunar glow of its glory light the tunnel so that they could see the way, but even as they reached the bent bars at the mouth of the tunnel below the city walls, Aphrodite descended wholly upon Odysseus and let her wrath kindle his jealousy until it, too, became a burning anger.

Finally, the jealousy became all-consuming, and as they slipped through the bars and into the overgrown trench Odysseus slipped the sword from his scabbard and raised it to strike Diomedes down, so that he might be the one to bear the palladium back to the lines of the Greeks.

Whether it was a warning from Athena or just mere happenstance, the light shining from the uncovered portion of the palladium glinted against Odysseus's raised sword blade and reflected into the trench ahead of Diomedes.

Immediately, Diomedes wheeled and was surprised to find his own brother-in-arms about to strike him down from behind. Reaching out, Diomedes caught Odysseus's wrist, arresting the downward swing of the blade that once belonged to the vaunted Achilles.

Diomedes twisted, prying the sword away from Odysseus's grip, so that it fell into the trench and was swallowed up by the muck. Still hanging on to Odysseus's wrist, Diomedes bent it back further, upending Odysseus and throwing him into the brambles at the side of the trench.

On the wall overhead, the Trojan guardsmen did not fail to hear the commotion. "Look there! A light among the brambles!"

The wall became a cacophony of shouts and warnings and a storm of spears descended through the overarching thicket, some caught in the tight press of foliage, but others penetrating and sticking deep in the earth of the trench.

Diomedes did not fail to see the madness that raged in Odysseus's eyes, and he reached for his own sword blade and struck Odysseus with the flat of it. "Take to your heels and get back to camp either before the Trojans skewer you, or before I forget all the times you saved my life and I yours and slay you for your treachery."

Odysseus hesitated for a moment, and Diomedes struck him again sharply, raising a welt on his forearm.

"Go!" snapped Diomedes. "Or I'll do the work of the Trojans for them and put you down like a mad dog!"

Spears and javelins continued to rain down upon the dense foliage, some slicing through as Odysseus lurched to his feet, past Diomedes, and down the trench.

Diomedes gave Odysseus another swat with the flat of his blade as he passed, and then he was hard on the heels of Odysseus, striking him with the flat of his blade whenever he would stumble or lag.

Leaving the shouts, curses, and hurtled javelins of the

Trojans behind they emerged from the trench and beat their way back to the Greek lines. It was only here that the wild-eyed lunacy that reflected in Odysseus's eyes finally diminished, and Aphrodite's dread influence fled to star-studded skies and back to the gibbous moon that shone overhead.

"Halt and identify yourselves," shouted the helmed guard from the palisades built from the lapped gunwales of Greek ships.

"We be Greeks: Diomedes and Odysseus."

"What are you doing outside the walls of our encampment?" called Paolimius, suspicion plain in his voice.

"We've raided the City of Troy and carried away its most precious possession."

"You claim to be Diomedes and Ulysses," challenged the sentry, "yet they are great warriors and wear the arms and armor of warriors. You wear the vestments of priests."

Diomedes tore away the robe. "Let us inside or I will climb the palisade and throw you to the Trojan dogs that are sure to be hounding our gates this very evening."

Even now, Paolimius was not convinced, for the moonlight was not sufficient to reveal the face of Diomedes to him. Other Greeks gathered round, readying their spears to cast them at the pair who had arrived at their gates. "Not even Diomedes and Ulysses could storm the walls of Troy by themselves and return alive," scoffed the Paolimius. "Show us this most precious possession stolen from the Trojans, and then mayhap I will believe that you are Diomedes and that whipped cur in front of you is Odysseus."

At this Odysseus seemed to completely emerge from the jealous trance which Aphrodite had laid upon him. He tore off his robe. "What did you call me?"

Paolimius felt safe on the height of the wall and still did not believe that this was Odysseus whose name he was impugning. "I called you a whipped cur. Now show us this precious treasure you claim to have stolen, else we skewer you with our spears."

"Avert thine eyes, or behold the glories of Athena's palladium!" Diomedes let the folds of the tapestry fall away from the personification of Athena on earth and all the true believers of the goddess were stunned by her ethereal pulchritude, so much that they fell back, shielding their eyes and others falling to their knees.

At this moment Odysseus launched himself at the palisade, his feet carrying him up the lapped wall so that he was able to reach out and grasp the gap between the crenellations. In but a moment, he hauled himself onto the top of the wall. Paolimius was gaping, in awe of the beauty that the palladium represented, and Odysseus grabbed him by the harness and hurled him over the side of the palisade. Bone crunched when Paolimius struck the earth, which had been packed hard by the tread of many sandals and much blood. Still, Paolimius lived, but as he attempted to rise Odysseus plucked away a spear from a stunned Greek and hurled it, pinning Paolimius through the chest and to the earth, so forceful was his throw.

Paolimius sank back to the earth, clutching at the shaft which pierced his chest, blood pouring from his mouth.

"Let that be a lesson to anyone who dare insult the name of Odysseus!" He roared from the wall.

Diomedes covered the palladium again and the Greeks cried out with victorious song that such a feat could be accomplished. That brave Greeks could creep into the very heart of the enemy's city and return with Athena's palladium. Even Menalaus in his far-flung pavilions heard the cheering and came to the walls accoutered in his silver-chased armor of bronze.

"What is the meaning of this?" demanded Menalaus.

"Tonight we have gazed upon two beauties," replied Odysseus. "We have seen the face of your lovely wife Helen, and we have witnessed the stunning beauty of Athena."

Menalaus seemed confused. "What are you saying, brother?"

"We have seized Athena's palladium, and we have even spoken with Helen this night."

"Is she well?"

"She is mournful," said Diomedes, "but her beauty and kindness remain unparalleled by any but Athena herself."

At first, Menalaus's expression was inscrutable, and then it turned to rage. "Why did you not bring Helen back instead of this cursed stick that the Trojan's worship?"

"Troy will fall now that the palladium is seized," said Odysseus. "The gods have guaranteed that. "You will possess Helen again, but for that to happen we needed the blessings and protections that the palladium will bring."

Menalaus's limbs trembled, but gradually his rage subsided. "You will receive much honor and glory upon your heads for this magnificent feat. I will pronounce three days of feasting to celebrate the arrival of the palladium in our camps! Now, I must go ponder our strategems to take the city of Troy."

When Menalaus and his guards had departed, Odysseus turned his gaze to Diomedes. "What did I do as we escaped Troy?" he spoke in low tones, so as not to be overheard by the lauding crowds.

"You went mad," answered Diomedes. "Mad as a rabid dog."

"I was jealous of the glories that you would receive, and I wanted to bear the palladium to our camp."

"You were going to stab me in the back!" said Diomedes. "It was only for the sake of the comradeship we once had that I didn't slay you when I had the chance."

"Forgive me," said Odysseus, the words nearly sticking in his craw, for he was a proud man. "It was a madness sent from the gods which came upon me. I had no control of my mind or limbs."

Diomedes considered this. "Once shattered, trust is a difficult thing to mend. Who is to say that this madness won't again descend upon you when my back is turned?"

For this, Odysseus did not have an answer. "The gods have long memories, Diomedes, and you have made enemies of at least two with your reckless deeds."

"Many of those reckless deeds have been performed with you guarding my side, brother Odysseus—but no longer. I fear that we must break our companionship."

Odysseus set his jaw. "Then we part as enemies?"

Diomedes shook his braided head. "Nay, though we part ways, never will a word of ill pass my lips in regards to the great Odysseus."

"Nor I in regards to the great Diomedes."

The two great warriors parted ways and returned to their pavilions. Diomedes set the palladium in the corner and for a long time sat upon his bench and contemplated the beauty of the goddess Athena. Then he covered her radiant glory with the same tapestry he had torn from the temple walls in Troy and retired to his bed, dreaming of his beloved wife Aegialeia and the time that they would be reunited.

109

About the Authors

D. ALAN LEWIS

In 1965, an object fell from space, somewhere near Kecksburg, PA. This was the same year that Alan was born. To date, no connection has been made between the two events but that hasn't stopped the conspiracy theorists from speculating.

D. Alan Lewis is an 'alleged' native of Chattanooga, Tennessee who now resides in Nashville with his children. He has been writing technical guides and manuals for various employers for over twenty years but only in recent years has branched out in to writing fiction. In 2006, Alan took the reins of the NWMG's Novelist Group where he works with new and aspiring writers.

Alan's debut novel, a fantasy murder mystery, *The Blood in Snowflake Garden* was a finalist for the 2010 Claymore Award. Lewis released two novels released in 2013, *The Lightning Bolts of Zeus* from Dark Oak and *The Bishop of Port Victoria* from Pro Se Press. He has also edited two anthologies for Dark Oak: *Capes & Clockwork* and the upcoming *Luna's Children*.

He also has short stories in a number of anthologies, including Dreams of Steam 4-Gizmos, Black Pulp, High Adventure History, and Midnight Movie Creature Feature Vol.2. On occasion, D. Alan Lewis also provides formatting services for Pro Se Productions.

PHILLIP DRAYER DUNCAN

Phillip Drayer Duncan is the author of *The First Chronicle of the Moonshine Wizard: A Fist of Thorns.* He was born in Eureka Springs, Arkansas and has spent most of his life in the Ozarks. He currently resides in Anderson, Missouri. Along with reading and writing like a madman, his passions include kayakin, canoein, fishin, shootin, video games, and pretty much anything nerd related. More than anything, his greatest passion includes spending time with his ridiculously awesome friends, his wonderful family, and his gorgeous girlfriend. Throughout the warm months, he can be spotted on the river, around a campfire, or at a concert. In the cold months, he can be found hermitting amongst a pile of books and video games. His greatest dream in life is to become a Jedi, but since that hasn't happened yet, he focuses on writing. His earliest books were written on notebooks, and acted out with action figures.

Phillip has written several stories for Pro Se, including a tale featuring his character, The Warden, in *Black Fedora*. He is currently writing a novel featuring The Warden.

JOEL JENKINS

Joel Jenkins is a Pulp Ark best author nominee and author of fifteen published novels and numerous short stories, including a children's book, genre fiction, and a biography. Jenkins lives with his wife and children in the misty, heron-haunted reaches of the Great Northwest, shadowed in the perpetual gloom of the Rainier Mountains. This former rock vocalist enjoys weightlifting, weapons collecting, and concocting a good tale.

PULSE-POUNDING PULP EXCITEMENT from AIRSHIP 27:

This is just a small sampling of the thrilling tales available from Airship 27 and its award-winning bullpen of the best New Pulp writers and artists. Set in the era in which they were created and in the same non-stop-action style, here are the characters that thrilled a generation in all-new stories alongside new creations cast in the same mold!

"Airship 27...should be remembered for finally closing the gap between pulps and slicks and giving pulp heroes and archetypes the polish they always deserved."
—William Maynard ("The Terror of Fu Manchu.")

PULP FICTION FOR A NEW GENERATION!
AT AMAZON.COM & WWW.AIRSHIP27HANGAR.COM

Made in the USA
Charleston, SC
13 April 2014